The Last Kiss

Also by Bruce Grant:

A Young Woman from China

Crossing the Arafura Sea

The
Last Kiss

BRUCE GRANT

Cover image by Fotolia © Yogesh More

Cover Design and typeset by BookPOD Pty Ltd

Printed and bound in Australia by BookPOD Pty Ltd

Typeset in Garamond Premier Pro 12/15

The poetry extracts from Vidyāpati are all from *Love
Songs of Vidyāpati*, translated by Deben Bhattacharya, edited
by W. G. Archer. part of a UNESCO series, George Allen
and Unwin, London, 1963. ISBN: 8120802926.

A Catalogue-in-Publication is available from
the National Library of Australia.

ISBN: 978-0-9925514-2-1
eISBN: 978-0-9925514-3-8

1

AT THE BOTTOM OF THE deep, enfolding garden was a pond with a fringe of eucalyptus trees. She strode towards it, away from the luminous house. She turned and walked backwards, watching the house leave her. It hovered above the darkness of the garden, buoyed by white pillars and coloured water sprinklers. She could see the people inside, sipping from fluted glasses, touching each other with the tips of their fingers, scanning with ravenous eyes. Their silhouettes through the French windows of the illuminated house were like a magic lantern show. Doomed!

She breathed deeply as she walked backwards, away from the big house. She could not stand the talk and tension, the twisting and twirling, slithering and shimmying. In a thousand years (if global warming, nuclear war or an asteroid did not wipe everyone out first) people like her would be studying their leftovers, their plastic cards, their coloured lenses, their lipsticks, their hearing aids, pacemakers and hip replacements. She could not stand them, so she just broke away, left them chattering their heads off like cockatoos.

She was wearing the wrong clothes for the brilliantly lit house. The grey silk dress clung to her body, showing how strong she was. The beads from the bazaar drooped in garish loops around her neck. Her basket-weave shoes, comfortable, brown, half-heeled, looked like squashed pumpkins on the polished floor. The floor was like a mirror, catching the glint of expensive clothes and the chandeliers overhead.

She turned her back on the floating house and strode towards the pond. She liked turning her back and walking away. It made her feel free.

She breathed in the warm air with its mysterious, cool layers. Moonlight from somewhere beyond the eucalypts made the garden glow. If she leaned over, she could see her face on the surface of the pond. She followed a broken-brick path on the edge of the water and stood in the enveloping darkness, listening to the creak of branches and the scuffle of insects in the twigs and bark on the ground. She brushed a mosquito away. The air was heavy in the cool of the garden. You had to keep reminding yourself that living in the heat could be managed, like everything else.

A man had been watching her from the time she had fled from the house, banging the door behind her. His skin was dark and his drab khaki uniform blended with him and the night, so she did not notice him, even when she reached the far side of the pond where he was standing. He stood behind her. He watched her open her purse and take out a packet of cigarettes, flick on a lighter, draw in greedily and exhale a fume of grey smoke. He could see the shape of her body against the illuminated house. He could see the outline of her legs and thighs through the flimsy dress. She tossed her head and he caught a glimpse of her profile. Her nose turned up slightly, giving a lift to her upper lip.

He was a man of quiet intensity, standing still and silent, watching her smoking, brushing back her short hair with the fingers of one hand, moving her hips as she shifted her weight from one foot to the other. He did not move. He controlled his breathing so that each intake was long and the air went down to his stomach. He was close enough to smell the smoke that had been in her mouth. She expelled it by pursing her lips, blowing it away from her little nose, which he imagined was lightly freckled. Her hair was probably brown. Freckles intrigued him, as someone from whose dark skin the sun's rays bounced ineffectually, and also, he noticed, those determined under hats and sunshades to remain incontrovertibly pale.

Her height was average. She would not be too tall for him. He imagined them standing, talking, one of her hands lightly touching his arm as she agreed with something he had said. She laughed as she glanced up at him and her laughter was like a password to a secret code.

A door of the house opened and four people, busy, merry, stepped outside, then hurriedly filed back, closing the door abruptly. She responded to the slap of the closing door by hunching her shoulders, feigning rejection. The blackness at the back of the pond closed in. The night became empty, the immense sky full of unknowable stars. She could hear the melancholy sound of distant traffic.

He moved one foot, not on the ground but within itself, easing his stance. He wriggled and flexed the fingers of one hand. The dull moonlight made the garden look like pressed metal, subdued, expectant. It was like Krishna and Radha at the lily pond. Her "partridge eyes", his "moon-fair face". He was so still he could scarcely breathe.

She tossed her cigarette away. With a shrug of irritation, she began to return to the house.

"That's one way to start a fire."

His voice was as calm and even as a light roller on a large lawn. It contained no heights, depths, nothing hidden, no currents, no edge. She knew he was not to be feared; he was just there, somewhere in the darkness, with his reassuring voice. His voice told her that he knew all the other ways to start a fire. He knew also about the illuminated house, the garden, the other houses and offices on the compound, the hotel built like a fortress on the corner, the other compounds in the diplomatic enclave.

"Sorry!"

They faced each other, but they could not yet see the expressions on their faces. He could see less of her now, with the illuminated house behind her. His outline became visible and she could make out his dark body and khaki clothes. Each waited, motionless, for the other's voice. Poised, still and silent. Then he coughed, as if apologising for his presence, and took a step in the direction of the tossed cigarette, practical, servant of law and order, searching with one leg among the twigs in the darkness for the smouldering butt, grinding it into the earth.

They were now side-on to each other, half-lit by the radiant residence and its spouting colours.

"A big party tonight."

He kept his eyes fixed on her face. She could see his eyes, which were calm and steady, like his voice. He saw from her eyes that she was in no hurry to leave the intimate world of the pond. She was more interested in him than the party in the pool of light.

"Very big. And very boring."

He nodded gravely. This was another aspect of the world he knew.

"And you?"

She wanted to know why he was alone in the darkness by the pond, although she knew before he answered that he had every right to be there. He had the look of someone entitled to be standing where he was, with the eucalyptus boughs sighing over his head. He explained that he was responsible for security and when there was a party in the floodlit house he would personally do the rounds.

"Just checking to see everything is alright."

"Good."

She adopted an air of authority, the source of which, however, needed explanation.

"I'm a guest here."

"I was told there was a guest."

That was another of the world's ways: to be told and not to know. A guest, but who, why and for how long? They liked to bring in outsiders from time to time, to liven things up. Not the other way around; they did not often move outside their own circle, where they were safe. In command. Sometimes the women ventured to the hills for a long weekend, or for a holiday abroad. Sometimes the men visited places where women, whose social or racial origins were not known or were not considered relevant, entertained them.

This woman. Was she different?

She could feel the tentative nature of this man, who knew how everything worked but did not control anything. She did not want to return to the big house, although by now her absence would have been noticed. Instead, she took a step towards him and lit another cigarette. She could see that his face was strong and humorous, unlined but not appealingly young, held in place by a body that seemed coiled to spring. He watched the lighter flick on, the red tip of the cigarette burn, the blue smoke coil and pour through her damp lips. She fumbled for the packet, squeezed it open with her thumb as she offered it to him. He declined with a fragile smile.

"Never, or just on duty?"

She seemed to want to make conversation, so he explained that he did not like to draw smoke into himself.

"In India fire is important," he said, and stopped short.

She considered what he had said, or might not have said, and responded abruptly. "Yes, it's a filthy habit." She tossed the cigarette away, laughed and stamped diligently at its smoke.

They faced each other like figurines, engaged and apart, motionless and ready, poised and counterpoised, seeing and not seeing. The vast night reared and soared above them. It was not an occasion for conversation. The dull glow of the garden asked them to be part of it, still and silent. Their eyes locked, level and lightly amused, while their bodies shadowed each other. He moved one leg, she moved one of hers, smiled. He smiled, eased one shoulder. She leaned slightly in response.

He could not believe his luck. He was standing watching the big house when this woman, with her gleaming white skin, appeared from nowhere. She came to him in the moonlight, like Radha. It must be a dream. But her body was near him, her smoky breath, her hot cheeks, her wet lips. And now, with a light smile, like a greeting, she placed a hand on his arm. He trembled with excitement, standing rigidly still. She mumbled some soothing words and drew back.

Suddenly, swiftly, he moved near to her, not touching, but near, very near. She quickly turned her head. The edges of their hands brushed, the smallest of his fingers touched, searched, their hands locked, pressed, levering her slowly around against him. She knew what he was doing and anticipated his movements. She did not fear this man. She knew from the beginning she had power over him.

Was it really happening? It was! He was so excited he could hardly breathe. He could get into trouble for this, serious trouble. But she, not he, was the one doing it, touching him like that. When their fingers locked, it was involuntary. He could say he was just steadying her. But he was entitled to respond. He was a man and she was a woman, even if she was a guest in the big house.

He closed his eyes for a moment to order his thoughts and … she touched him again! Two, perhaps three, firm, confident fingers were touching his thigh. He had to respond. This was once in a lifetime. She was Radha. He was Krishna. At the lily pond! In the moonlight! He turned to her, his face taut as if he were being tested, as if meeting a great challenge in his life.

So it was that Annie, an Australian archaeologist who had come to India to make some preliminary studies of the Harappan civilisation, and Gopala, an Indian poet who made a living working in the Australian high commission, became lovers.

2

She needs to explain at the residence why she will be staying in India longer than expected. She had planned for two weeks, long enough to do some research, attend a conference, have a bit of a holiday. Now she is wondering if she can stretch it to three weeks. Maybe four. She mentions this to her host and hostess at the breakfast table in elusive sentences containing unfamiliar and untruthful words. Her project is proving to be more complex – and more rewarding and fascinating – than she had expected. It is moving in unexpected directions, leading her into uncharted waters, opening up unknown territory. It had started as a small, personal interest; now it was taking on the character of something, well, more important.

Porridge, which she has never eaten before. Thin half-slices of toast in a silver frame. Mangoes cut on the skin so that they unfold in your mouth like pollen spores at the centre of a flower. Thick, black coffee with frothing milk poured at a distance from a copper jug. They nod helpfully, trapped in formality, enmeshed in busyness. She can stay as long as she likes. She is the daughter of old friends. Her project seems to be held in high regard. It could turn out to have national, or even international, significance. And kindly pass the toast.

Annie telephones home. Listening to the tinkling-bell tone, she imagines the scene: if her mother is not in the kitchen to answer, her father will have to come in from the back, where he is probably watering the geraniums, deadheading the camellias or scraping moss from the brick path. He would wipe his boots on the mat provided, park his garden tools near the kitchen door and slowly enter.

"Yeah?" He sounds annoyed at being interrupted. She was inexplicably filled with joy.

"Dad, it's me."

"Oh, yeah. How's it going? Something wrong?"

"Well, no, I was just checking to see if you were alright."

"We're fine. Nothing going on here."

"That's good."

"What's the weather like over there?"

"Well, it's very different. But I'm getting used to it."

"When're you coming home?"

"Well, that's it. I thought I might stay a bit longer. Two or three weeks."

"Good."

"Well, I'd better get going. Glad everything's alright." A pause in which the distance between Australia and India seemed suddenly immense. "Just wanted to hear your voice."

"Oh, yeah. Just the same, cranky as ever."

"OK, better get off."

"Yeah, don't want to break the bank chinwagging."

"No. Give my love to Mum."

"Right."

They hang up, both thinking that nothing had changed.

She goes out into the hot sun, wearing her tennis hat for protection, pretending to talk to the gardener about pruning roses. She smells the flowers, fingers them for texture, observes the shape of the stems, kicks at the soil. The gardener, who has been all his working life at the house and has lately begun to believe that its inmates, who change every three years or so, are not interested in having a floral display announcing his retirement, which he secretly desires, mistakes her for an enthusiast. He tells her the history of the rose bushes, which had been brought from Canberra, while her eyes search the compound.

She hangs around the sweepers brushing the paved courtyard with their wisps of brooms, and then wanders back to the gardener to remark on the weather and ask why even non-deciduous trees are losing their leaves. She strolls over to the garage, commenting to the drivers on the sheen of the cars.

Then she sees him. He is standing in the shadows of an ashok tree. The sunlight glints through the long, shiny, narrow leaves with wavy edges, daubing him with gold. The air is breathless. The tree and the man stand motionless together, like a pair of sentinels. She waves at him but he does not notice, or respond.

That night, as she prepares to go to bed, she notices a pink slip of paper protruding from beneath the pillow. On it is written:

"Radha, you are an ocean of nectar
And Krishna is afloat in it
Like a furious elephant."

Furious elephant! How did he get into her room? She had never seen him in the house. He must have an associate, a fellow conspirator, probably the servant who turned down all the beds at the same time each day. Wheels within wheels.

They meet in the maze of hedges that separate the cottages on the compound. The hedges have grown scraggly and do not screen them completely, so they are careful not to show any intimacy. Even so, with her eyes demurely lowered, she moves one sandalled toe bit by bit on the gravel path until it encounters a shining shoe. When they look at the pond, they remember its secret.

They speak only of practical things, like the arrangements for their meetings. He tells her when he will be free to meet her at the bungalow. It is not wise to use the telephone.

"In India, all sorts of people listen to telephone conversations."

The words hover in the air, accompanied by his rubbery smile.

"You mean the operator?" There is a central exchange at the high commission.

"Not just the operator, all sorts of people. You have a mobile phone?"

"Of course."

"Don't use it for anything you don't want people to know. Turn it off when we're talking. It's like a microphone. You've heard of eve-teasing?"

She nods. The first advice she was given at the residence was not to use public transport, because the men deliberately squeezed themselves against you. That was eve-teasing, one of India's national pastimes.

"Another is eaves-dropping." He chortles at his witty play with Indian duplicity and the English language.

He plans each meeting as if it is a military operation. She leaves the residence at 1630 hours, reaches the library at 1642 hours (where the residence thinks she is going), circles for three minutes (or, alternatively, parks and enters for a maximum of five minutes overall), arriving at the bungalow between 1659 and 1704 hours. Her scornful laugh stops him. She does not need to obey the wily rules of Indian assignations. She can go to and from the residence when she feels like it, her back straight, her skirt raised to her knees, her strong white legs pushing at the pedals. He might know what goes on in the residence, but he does not know its nature, nor hers.

Sometimes she wears slacks or jeans, but she likes the freedom of a skirt, the air circulating under it like butterflies. She borrows a man's bicycle from the servants, without the lowered bar in the middle; mounting and dismounting is cumbersome, but she brushes aside his comment. People do not gather to look when she is mounting. Only the servants are there and, in any case, she uses steps to give her height. She rides straight to the bungalow or if she does stop at the library, she uses the front steps to dismount, entirely decorously. No one tries to look under her skirt. He growls impassively.

She wears a tennis hat with a floppy brim to protect her face from the sun he ignores. As she does not normally wear hats, it keeps slipping so she often squashes it into the carrier. Her story at the residence is that she bicycles each day to the library. No one from the residence ever goes there; just in case, she carefully cycles near the library, with her hat off, available to be seen. On days they are not able to meet, she goes inside, takes a book from the shelves and sits for a while reading.

She explains her library visits in detail to the servants, knowing they will spread the word. What was she reading? Not just books but also historical documents that were only released on inter-library loan after approval from high up. Sometimes she sat in the main reading room with the general public, but she also had a room of her own in another part of the building. The residence passes her words around. Her desire for scholarship and her pleasure in bicycling are topics of conversation. It shows respect for Indian culture, doesn't it, going to a library? And her bicycling shows that she is not afraid to go about her business like any young Indian woman, not cooped up in a chauffeur-driven, air-conditioned car. Just another human being in the great river of life. Indians liked that. She was engaged on a serious project. Indeed, she was a serious, interesting person, which reflected well on the residence, didn't it? The words ping-ponged on social occasions in the big house.

She parks her bicycle at the side of his bungalow, a small, upright, desolate building, surrounded by an indeterminate lawn and an inflorescent garden in the middle of a large, flat block of land. The path from the gate is lined with stones dabbed white on top, as in Indian military camps. A servant watches her arrive. Some children from other bungalows materialise. She smiles, claps her hand on theirs. Tea and cake are served as soon as she arrives. She sits sedately sipping tea and nibbling cake. Then the servant clears away and, like starving animals, they fall upon each other on the big teak bed.

In the bungalow are his poems, cries of sadness and longing, also funny. Sometimes, they litter the big teak bed when they make love. Occasionally, one will slip or float to the floor. He gathers them up later without comment and places them in a neat pile, ready for work. They are in Hindi script. A fragment in English catches her eye, but the phrases are disjointed, the words frequently amended, written at angles across the page or cramped into spaces in corners or between lines.

"Have you had anything published?"

"Published?"

He is tongue-tied with modesty or embarrassment, or perhaps the effort required to conceal an ambition to be India's greatest poet.

"Recently?"

She wants to make her own assessment, but his poetry isn't written in English. He is sensitive, so she doesn't press him. Publication wasn't that important, anyway. You never got even near the truth in public. If you said in public how you really felt or what you really thought, people would think you were from outer space.

Lurking in his grave manner is an unpredictable sense of humour. After a particularly solemn pronouncement, he will dance, coiling himself into a knot, then extruding a face like a burnished coin, revealing in some small detail, such as a twitch at the corner of his mouth or one slightly raised eyebrow or a forehead that rises in furrowed waves above itself, a comment on the vast reality outside that was sometimes life and sometimes India. In the garden of the residence in his khaki clothes that were not really a uniform, but looked like one, he was erect and slow-moving, as if his authority needed a presentation. In the bungalow he skips, tumbling like a furry animal, spins like a dancer, and then, with a slow, sad, dazzling smile, flops down beside her.

He tells her that when he saw her in the darkness at the pond, he thought she was Radha. She scoffs. Does that make him Krishna, India's most popular deity? He lowers his eyes in silence.

"You really think you're Krishna? Just because your mum gave you one of his names."

He remains silent. Well, she thinks, why not, if you believe in reincarnation. But she needs to make her own position clear. "Let me tell you something. I'm not Radha." She does not know what she means, but grins at him to make sure he catches her mood.

He speaks of his childhood, how he had been brought up, fed, suckled and comforted by a servant, who sang him lullabies and told him stories of old India. His father worked in a store, guarding the till; his mother taught at a primary school and sewed. It was the servant who cuddled him. Annie wonders what she would have been like if she had been brought up by a servant, kissed and cuddled by a warm, guiltless woman.

The heat in the middle of the day is fierce, like fire; she has to lower her head against it. Inside, his bungalow is as breathless as an oven. She feels sometimes she must cut the air with a knife to make a pocket in which to breathe. He had inherited a fan with the bungalow, but was reluctant to use it. His father had told him that illnesses were caused by bloodstreams upset by bubbles of unexpected air; waves of air entered your body and disturbed your bloodstream. She insists. She even implies that without the fan she might not be amenable to him on the big teak bed, although they both know this is not true. Her cooperation on the bed is a foregone conclusion. Still, he switches on the fan for her, after turning it so that it does not blow directly on them. It has a nick on one of the blades and hums with a snarl that becomes a growl when it slows. The power often fails, leaving the room eerily quiet.

She has never felt so desirable before. He is like a puppy, licking bits of her, wriggling for her affection. His technical knowledge is impressive. Sometimes, as she sets out for his bungalow, she gives a little shiver of excitement. "I wonder what it will be today."

Before, the emotion of lovemaking had been important. Sensual pleasure flowed like a river once its emotional source was tapped. Love would find a way. Without it, no detail was satisfying in itself, a dry twig on a green bough. Now, all the twigs came to life. Each part of her body was manipulated with fine precision, this way, that way. She lies on her back, on one side and the other, on her front, under him and on top of him, back to front and front to back. She opens her legs, bends her knees, arches her back, lifts her rump, twists her shoulder. He does not say anything; his touch and his pressure tell her what to do.

They contain themselves while the servant serves tea, sitting upright opposite each other. He gulps at his cup and tears a corner off his cake to show that the ritual of tea is not the farce it is, but even as they sit pretending, she eases a foot from its shoe and pushes her bare toes between his thighs and he leans across and strokes his fingers along her leg, while balancing his cup with his other hand. As soon as the servant closes the door, he grasps her hand and twists her against him, as he had done at the pond, and she submits to the swift plunge and press of his body.

Sometimes, they do not quite make it to the bed. They tumble from their chairs, crawling over the floor like jungle fighters, pushing away furniture to make room for their exertions, grabbing at cushions to give them leverage and comfort. Afterwards, they flop on the bed to rest.

The marks of love show for days. The bruises, the bites. She covers them with long sleeves, high collars and foundation cream, but languorous eyes, deeply satisfied, persist. The distracted mind is everywhere, its antennae

17

broken. She tries to cover her distracted state by being bright and cooperative, but she cannot keep it up. Sensible explanations, in which cause and effect are neatly joined, become feats of ingenuity. Silence absorbs the middle of conversation. Hot flushes. Daily routines are followed as if in a dream.

They never go anywhere or do anything together. He never takes her to a restaurant, to see a film, nor even just to take a walk together. He does not have a car. The idea of taking a drive with him makes her smile. He is not the sort for an afternoon spin in the country. She cannot imagine him behind a driving wheel, except perhaps in a state of serene and dangerous detachment. Still, she could drive.

"Why don't we go for a picnic?"

His face flashes with childlike excitement, and then subsides.

"Picnic?"

"Yes. I'll make up a hamper." She stops speaking while she thinks about the food they could take. "There's tons of luncheon stuff at the residence. They're always making up picnic baskets for guests, who go to some river and sit on the bank under shade trees. They say peacocks fly over your head."

He seems to be considering the prospect.

"I'll hire a car," she says.

He purses his lips and wriggles his head slightly. His mind is roaming far and wide. "Let me think about it."

"I'll drive."

His eyes light up. That seems to take one corner of the weight from his mind. Perhaps he has never learned to drive. He nods heavily. "Let me think about it."

She suggests that he might like to swim with her in the pool in the big government hotel near the compound, to which she has access.

"Would that be wise?"

All the unanswerable questions about India are contained in his quest for wisdom. She is never sure of his mood. Sometimes, he speaks of India as if it were undergoing a great social experiment in the vanguard of human progress. Sometimes, he speaks as if it always has been and always would be a pit of iniquity and futility. Nothing can change it. Then his voice becomes sad and flat: this unchangeable quality is a tragedy. At other times, he speaks as if it is India's strength, protecting the people against evils and uncertainties, absorbing social change and economic development without diluting the eternal essence of India.

"My father told me never to trust a Thakur."

He explains that Thakurs are upper-caste Hindus in his village. His father knew how much land each person owned in his village and how much was owned by outsiders. He knew how everyone in the village voted at elections. He was expert at detecting spite, eloquent at explaining hatred, a connoisseur of fear and envy. He was also a man of action. He had organised the dairymen in his state to protest against a new policy.

His father did not approve of foreigners. Bifurcation was dangerous. To grow serenely, the tree of life must have a single trunk.

Annie expected Gopala to twist his lips to distance himself from his father's words, but he doesn't. What his father said stood as he had said it. His father spoke as if an iron law governed India's destiny. His mind found certainty in numbers. He thought that it took a thousand years for something new to become established.

"My father does not trust Muslims. They have been in India only since the 13th century," Gopala said sternly.

His father had told him when he was a boy that the number five was important. Gopala looked sideways at Annie. "There are five organs of the senses and five organs of action." He listed them methodically. Eyes, ears, tongue, nose, skin. And: hands, feet, mouth, anus, penis. His father had worked out that every sexual act could be performed in multiples of four.

Annie does not care about the father. He is a disembodied voice to which she listens only because the son speaks on his behalf. What she wants is the man who is always waiting for her in the gloom of his bungalow and the energy that leaps at her when she enters the room.

He comes from a village near Patna in the state of Bihar. She comes from a suburb of Melbourne, in the state of Victoria. She does not talk about her family. He never asks, so she does not offer. At times, when he mentions something about himself, he pauses, as if the next step would be to inquire whether it is the same in her family, but she does not take the hint. Family talk is boring, people trying to make something of themselves. She does not want him to think about anything or anyone except her.

She can tell from the way he looks at her that he regards her as a prize. This is what the fight for national independence was for, this is what really counts – not the statistics of growth and per capita this and gross national product that, not justice and equality and the abolition of poverty, prejudice and the disgraceful, stubborn customs of caste, religious patriarchy and widow-burning, but the universal, irreducible, racial equality of the bed. In multiples of four.

Is she also enslaved? His skin is so black that at times it shines like a suit of armour, and he is like another kind of man inside it. The men she has known needed to be approached as if she were aware of their personalities and sensitive to their needs. You kept conscientiously somewhere in the back of your mind the possibility of a more substantial relationship, even mutual responsibilities. Now she is without conscience. She has no idea what this man needs or wants, likes or dislikes, apart from the obvious. His energy wells up inside him from sources unknown to her.

She knows almost nothing about him, whether he is for or against globalisation and the war against terrorism, his attitude to global warming, whether he enjoys cricket, what food he likes, what shaving cream he uses. She does not feel the need to find out. He satisfies her the way he is. He is like an emissary from an unknown land, with pieces of vital information that are available to her only as he feels inclined to release them. The whole can never be known, not because it is a secret but because it is so vast. He is a humble servant of this known unknown. His personal needs are like a grain of sand in a desert.

She is drawn to him as she is drawn to adventure, breaking out, getting away, seeing the world. Having sex with a stranger was the ultimate freedom. Giving yourself in the most intimate way you can to someone who has no idea who you are or what you are like, who isn't attracted to you for any particular aspect of your looks or personality, or what you do or your prospect as a lifelong partner, but who wants you desperately because you were born with a white (pink, really) skin, was the most complete break you could make with the loving paraphernalia of life.

Away with tenderness!

She comes across a print from a painting in one of the Ajanta caves. It shows a group of women clustered around an elegant and contemplative male figure, the whole composition expressing grace and composure. The lascivious faces of the women take her breath away. She is startled and then intrigued by the picture, and also by the inscription on the wall of the cave: "Blossoms are the ornaments of trees, flashes of lightning colour the rain clouds, the lakes are adorned by lotuses and waterlilies with their intoxicated bees; but virtues brought to perfection are the proper ornaments of living beings."

Virtue? There was nothing virtuous in the jewelled flesh of these women of Ajanta.

"The Ajanta caves were cut from the western ghats over a period of hundreds of years, beginning before the Christian era," Gopala informed her.

"These caves were supposed to be monasteries," she informed him in return. "But those wall paintings. Boy!"

"Buddhist," he said, as if that were answer enough.

"But how did Buddhist monks manage to surround themselves with gorgeous girls like that?"

"Self-denial. And compassion. That was Buddha's message."

Annie's voice was slashed with scorn. "Those faces are seething. Call it what you like, it's not denial."

Gopala was lost in contemplation of the man at the centre of the ornamental cluster. "The man is seeking virtue," he said primly. "The women are the ornaments."

Annie was in exposure mode. "Let me tell you, they're not ornaments. And his compassion is having a bad effect on them."

"Perhaps it is art, not history," suggested Gopala. "The use of colour. Those yellow and brown ochres for the skin, the lamp black for the hair – they make the women strong. The man is in white dhoti, with a lapis lazuli patina on the wall behind him."

Annie chortled: "Art or history, the effect is the same. He might be gaining virtue for a future life, but those girls are heading in another direction." She pointed dramatically at the floor. "Down!"

"The Hindu way is better." Gopala spoke with a barely perceptible wobble of his head.

"You mean all the things the Buddhists tried to get rid off, like widow-burning and caste?"

"No, I mean the woman as active partner." He turned his eyes to her with a sly smile. "Coitus in the reverse position."

She knows what he means, although she had not known it was exclusively Hindu.

"My father says no Muslim will do it. Muslims believe that if a child is born this way, it will have a squint."

She might have been an angel, under the personal protection of the virginal Mary, for all the interest he showed in her virtue. When she asks him to use a condom, he protests with taut face and straining eyes, as if she is destroying his inner being. He explains that Indians believe the mind controls the body. He describes the fertility cycle and the philosophy of the deferred good, in which satisfaction postponed is pleasure prolonged. She insists they take precautions. This is India. She isn't that crazy.

"It's not natural."

"It's better than the acquired immune deficiency syndrome."

"I don't have AIDS!"

"Of course not. But perhaps I do."

"But we've already ..." His voice fades into silence. "What is the point?"

She does not know the technical answer, or even if there is one. She is sure that his shining black statue body does not harbour diseases, and it certainly is difficult to accomplish the task of fitting a condom on efficiently, even to remember to do it, when they are falling over each other on the big teak bed. Also, if he won't provide them, how will she? Where do you get them in India?

He looks at her with a kind of blank despair. She is determined. So he submits, dismissing her anxiety about the Indian product.

"India makes very good condoms," he says sternly, as if defending his country's nuclear deterrent.

She sometimes experiences waves of sadness after lovemaking. Not immediately afterwards, when she lies fizzing with pleasure, but when he is sleeping and she watches the light through the slats coming into the room. The sadness creeps over her like unsettled weather, an uneasy wind, a flushed sky, a heavy cloud. She had read somewhere that making love during the day had this effect. Was it that?

Or was it that the live statue, strong and hard, was without feeling? He never shows any tenderness, never kisses her lips. Whatever he feels is slotted into something that is always there, outside himself, waiting, like an automatic bank machine. He presses the button and the machine whirrs and clicks into life. Whirr! Click! When it is over, he becomes human and humorous again. Or falls asleep.

She wonders whether it is possible ever to have enough of this magnificent probing and thrusting. She wonders whether she can live forever on this high ridge between pleasure and pain. Her relief at these times is also disappointment that her expectations have had to come to a delicious conclusion. Perhaps that explained the sadness.

The best way to break the sadness was to swing herself off the bed, wash in the rudimentary bathroom with its smell of wet tin and cement, and walk out. Sometimes she would be gone before he woke but usually he stirred as she was leaving and she would stand still in the middle of the room, waiting for him to acknowledge her departure. He farewelled her formally. Namaste! Behind the raised and pointed hands of the Indian salute, his eyes glittered, his lips pursed playfully and his head swayed slightly.

Once he turned his black back on her, trapped in sleepiness.

She thinks that if she can understand him, she will understand India. In him is distilled the residue of hundreds, thousands of years of intense heat, torrential rain, sumptuous riches, cruel poverty, political murder and mayhem, discovery and romance, failure and ruin. He is its essence. His long silences are like still, deep water, his voice is like a mountain piper's tune, connecting random bits of mysterious knowledge. He is a poet who is part of a remorselessly poor and practical system. In his bungalow are books, reading lamps, posters, but also old wooden furniture and worn linoleum, tubular steel, drums and cans, webbing. He is like a statue, worn and marked, touched but unchanged by events, permanent.

At the market she buys a small temple piece (early 18th century they said, but she buys it anyway for the way it fits into her hand), its face worn by millions of fingers, its body smooth and hard. She carries it with her to hold and touch when they are apart.

"Australia is part of Asia," she informs him one day.

He sees a woman with freckles and a small, upturned nose, a wrinkle in her neck when her head moves quickly, her hair in a flustered bun. Her blue-green eyes are direct, daring him. He turns the idea over slowly, his face vacant.

Actually, she does not believe Australia is part of Asia. She cannot stand Australians who go around yapping about "engagement" or "enmeshment" with Asia and what it really means to be an Australian. Some even talk about a "national identity". It was just a confidence trick. Australia didn't have a national identity or if it did, no one knew what it was. It could be anything. It depended on what happened – who won and who lost, how clever people were, what they did with their lives. There were lots of identities. The Oz-identity floggers were themselves at sixes and sevens, because they didn't know what Australians were for or against.

The idea that Australia was "part of Asia" used to upset the greybeards when everyone was British to the bootstraps, and then all the way with the Yanks, but now everything was such a jumble that Australia wasn't part of anything except the human race. Australians had to strip down and do their own thing, relying on professional people like herself to give them the facts. Great! History was just another con, made up by people who liked the way things had turned out. You never knew until you dug it up, actually held something in your hand that had really existed. The old man was right. A thousand years at least.

No one in Australia knew how she was supposed to behave. Great!

So why bother to raise the silly topic with Gopala, when she didn't believe what she said? Well, she didn't want him to think that she was only interested in sex and, just because she was in his country, didn't have any rights.

3

Annie was cycling in circles in front of the library near Jor Bagh Road with her hat off, not knowing whether to go back to the residence for lunch or visit one of the nearby markets, when a boy ran out thrusting a piece of paper at her. On it was a handwritten request to telephone the residence urgently. She parked her bicycle and taking the piece of paper to the library office asked the girl at the counter if she could use the telephone. Of course. They had been waiting for her. They had been looking all over the library for her. The residence said she had a special room; she was working on some historical documents.

The girl was articulate and charming. It was not expected, or necessary, that she should have been told about the special room. A lot went on in her building, such a busy place. She was not expected to know everything. The girl waved her hands and wriggled her glossy head, simulating the endless possibilities of life at the library.

"How did you find me?"

"One of the sentries had noticed you on your bicycle."

"How long were you trying to find me?" Annie asked, managing the urgency in her voice.

The girl set about preparing an explanation. "Well ..." she said, glancing at her watch.

She was not confident with the question of time. She peered into the middle distance. She glanced again at her watch. "Not very long."

"Never mind."

The telephone at the residence was persistently engaged, so she decided to ride back and clear up the matter on the spot. The girl at the counter hoped everything would be alright. She was pleased they had found her so quickly. She was proud of her role. "I wrote the note."

It was something to do with the office, the servants told her. She had to see Mr Gleeson, whom she did not like. His neat, methodical body was forbidding. His eyes were as shallow as slate. His language was abstract and deferential. She had spoken to him about using the bicycle, which was supplied for the servants' use but rarely used, and he had tried to convince her that it was not safe (or perhaps he meant ladylike) to ride bicycles built for men. Mr Gleeson managed to imply, without saying anything to which exception could be taken, that he did not trust you.

But it was cool in his air-conditioned offices. While she waited, she turned the pages of dog-eared magazines with pictures of glazed women and their muscled men at play on Australian beaches.

A secretary opened a door and invited her to enter. Mr Gleeson was not alone. There were four other men, two she recognised from the compound and two Indians in some kind of uniform. Mr Gleeson was all smiles as she entered, beaming with friendliness as he offered her a seat. "Cigarette?"

He fumbled with a silver box on his desk but she declined. The others resumed their seats. In a surprising display of informality, Mr Gleeson moved to the front of his desk and propped himself against it. He was wearing a white shirt with long sleeves and a blue tie with a sporting-club or old-school insignia and he folded his arms impressively. He looked at her with intense interest, as if he were about to announce that she had won a prize.

"We are sorry to bother you, but, as you will see, something important has come up," he said. He nodded vigorously to give emphasis to what he had said. "Something important."

The other men shifted uneasily in their seats, but withheld whatever they were thinking. Mr Gleeson reached behind himself and took from his desk a piece of paper that he studied carefully.

"You expect in a society like India what I will call slippage, or perhaps bleeding or leaching is a better description. The slow wastage of assets. It cannot be helped. It is accepted." He was determined to make the point more precisely. "You budget for it. How much? It varies from year to year. It is a matter of judgment. Some people in my position have made that judgment as low as one or two per cent. Some have gone as high as five or seven per cent. It depends on a whole set of circumstances, including, may I say, the degree of cooperation we receive from our friends, the Indian police."

The two outsiders acknowledge his interest by minutely inclining their heads.

"So we are not unrealistic. We don't set ourselves the same standard we would back home. At the same time, we can't ignore what is staring us in the face." He looked intently at her. "Staring us in the face." As she did not like Mr Gleeson, she quickly tired of his introduction to whatever it was that she had been brought back to be told. She nodded impatiently.

"I am setting the scene," he explained. "I want you to be completely reassured, absolutely sure that our motives in this are of the highest possible order." He examined her features as if he were searching for something. "Completely reassured. In your own mind."

He was searching for her mind, she thought, and giggled. Mr Gleeson noticed. He walked around his desk and sat in his chair. He gathered together more pieces of paper. "I raise this matter in the strictest confidence."

She listened with mounting horror as he explained that they had become aware, indicating the four other men, that for some time a certain person who had a position in the compound's security unit had been lingering at the compound outside his hours of duty. "Lingering. Outside hours of duty." This man was now the prime suspect in their investigations into the theft of petrol supplies. "The prime suspect." A couple of drivers were also involved, but he was the instigator. "Instigator." He had been confronted with the evidence, which was overwhelming. "Overwhelming." But his defence was that on each occasion when he had filled a tank outside office hours, he had been authorised to do so by someone at the residence. "Someone at the residence." When asked for proof, he said that the authority was verbal, not in writing. "Verbal." When asked who had verbally given him the authority, he said it was … Mr Gleeson paused. Then, examining Annie's face carefully as if seeing it for the first time or making sure that its owner was actually in his office, continued, "Your good self.

"Your good self. So you can see why we needed your kind assistance. Kind assistance. The police would like to make an arrest now. Now. But I thought it only fair to acquaint you with what is being contemplated. It is more than probable that, after he is arrested, the person in question will repeat his claim that you authorised him to take the petrol. Repeat his claim."

Mr Gleeson's humourless eyes offered no guide to the direction of his thoughts, but Annie knew what he wanted. He wanted to co-opt her in asserting his authority over Gopala. He also wanted to cover his back from any possible reaction at the residence.

"What are you asking me to do?"

"We are not asking anything, dear lady." He was appalled at the thought. "We are asking nothing. Nothing at all."

She gathered herself together, preparing to leave. Mr Gleeson stood up.

"It would complete our inquiries usefully, however, if you could state, in your own language, of course, but leaving no doubt as to your meaning, that at no time did you authorise him to take the petrol. At no time."

He smiled around the room, as if he had disposed of a disagreeable matter in an effective, administrative manner. As Annie did not respond, he dropped his smile and fingered his tie.

"You understand, of course, that there is a padlock on the petrol pump in the compound for which only two keys are held. Only two. One is held by the gentleman in question and the other is held by myself. He does not dispute that he released the petrol. Does not dispute. He simply claims to have been authorised to do so by your good self. Your good self. So, if you state categorically that you did not, that will be the end of it. And, I should think, the end of him."

After what was evidently his last word, he returned to his sociable stance at the front of his desk, arms folded.

Her answer came like bullets directed at Mr Gleeson's plump, insistent body. As she fired, he staggered, crumpled, went behind his desk to sit in his chair. The Indian policemen lowered their eyes in deference to the extremity of their colleague's distress.

In short, sharp sentences that could not be misinterpreted, she said that, of course, she had authorised the person in question to release the petrol.

The phrase reverberated in her head and she could not resist repeating it. "Release the petrol!" And before anyone could ask her why, she smiled at the other four men and stalked from the room.

Walking back to the residence, she asked herself why on earth she had done it. She knew, of course; it was to spite the Gleesons of this world. But how could she explain herself to her hosts, who were part of the same world? And why had Gopala used her name? Had he told the despicable Gleeson what happened at the pond? Surely not, but cornered, he might have.

Nothing was said to her at the residence. Her host and hostess behaved normally, asking at breakfast how the project was going, listening dutifully to her answers and, as always, conscientious and cheerful about their appointment-filled days. The servants fussed over her as usual. And the ominous Gleeson went benignly about his business on the compound without another word to her, as if nothing had happened. Should she approach him?

"By the way, Gleeson, I would like to confirm that our conversation the other day about that important matter was conducted in the strictest confidence, as you explicitly said, and that you will honour that understanding, as of course, on my side, I intend to do." She giggled, slapping him on the shoulder. "Old chap!"

She wondered seriously what Mr Gleeson might do. He would not give up, that was certain. He might drop the charges, but he would not give up. He would not be happy with wastage or leakage or leaching or whatever it was at whatever percentage he thought it was. She wondered what his acceptable level of human corruption might be. He would certainly not give up on moral frailty in the compound. What about moral frailty outside the compound? She gauged his strengths and weaknesses. His strength was his narrow-minded efficiency. His weakness was his awe of authority. He would inform the residence, of course.

She watched his office building from her bedroom balcony. She saw men going in and coming out. Cars and trucks lined up at the petrol pump. Disconnected voices floated over the trees like the cries of birds. Vultures circled in a white-hot sky. A heat haze hovered above the pond at the bottom of the garden.

She heard her name being called insistently from somewhere. From the bottom of the stairway, her hostess's upturned face posed a lengthy question.

"Would you like to come with us this long weekend to a place we've got in the hills. Mussoorie. It'll do you good. Cool air. Pleasant walks. That sort of thing. Don't worry, we'll leave you alone to work on your project, if that's what you want. We hardly talk to each other up there. Just read, sleep and go for walks. At the most, table tennis and Scrabble." Her hostess paused, but apparently still wondered if she was making her invitation clear. "You'll like it. It's a bit of India you should see. Hill station, that sort of thing."

Annie was quiet, thinking of being alone in the house. But with servants you were never alone.

"Come on, Annie. Say yes. You'll love it."

"Yes, of course."

She was determined to see him before she went, so she strode across the lawn, through the rose garden and found him talking with the drivers at the garage. He detached himself from the drivers as she approached.

"Hello, furious elephant," Annie said. She told him that they must meet, urgently.

He inclined his head, but his smile, inward and satisfied, denied deference. He simply said, "1650 hours."

"God only knows what you're doing," she told him at the bungalow, "but I supported you." She shrugged. "Well, it's only petrol. You would think from the way Gleeson carried on that you were pinching India's foreign currency reserves."

"It wasn't a full tank," he said carefully. "It was just topping up. I mentioned your name because I thought that would put an end to it. I never expected it to get this far."

"It was more than once, from what Gleeson said. It goes on all the time. A couple of drivers are also involved."

The information rolled over his hunched shoulders and downcast eyes. He was away in imponderable India. "The drivers can use the cars for other purposes. Makes them a few rupees." The detail seemed to sadden him. "Or they can siphon the petrol out again, and sell it. It's nothing. It's about what they would spend at the residence on tea and biscuits for guests. Everyone does it. The servants at the residence cream a bit off everything all the time. The drivers expect it. Even the gardeners."

He raised his head and fixed his eyes on her. "It's the Indian way."

"And, in return, the drivers do something for you?"

He moved his head slowly from side to side, which she took to suggest that, while the answer was technically in the affirmative, the transactions were so small as to be barely visible to the naked eye. He strengthened his position by pointing out that foreigners like Gleeson were paid much more than his Indian counterparts. Also, the compound got supplies cheaper than Indians through tax concessions for diplomats. So it was reasonable that Indians working for these foreigners should be able to spread the benefits among themselves and, through them and their families, to the general community.

It seemed reasonable to her. "But next time you might warn me before you take my name in vain." She looked at him steadily. "And you said nothing about us?"

He shook his head. She saw the surprise in his eyes that she could even have thought he might have told Gleeson about the pond.

"But you did," he said.

She was about to deny that she had done anything of the sort, when she realised he might be right. Gleeson had no understanding of the reason for her false, provocative statement that she had authorised Gopala to take the petrol, but he had the kind of mind that would jump to the conclusion she was shielding a lover. What other reason could she have had? By stalking out, she had not given him an opportunity to explore other possibilities.

Their relationship changed that evening. She had released not only the petrol, but also Gopala with it. They were lovers now, free and equal. She was scared, knowing that the unspeakable Gleeson would make the most of her indiscretion, but she also felt strong. She took the lead in their lovemaking. She did not bother to ask him to turn on the fan. Her eyes were stretched wide, her arms rigid on his heaving chest.

"My horse, my horse!"

When it was over, he observed her under heavy eyelids and slowly recited:

"Her hair, dishevelled,

31

Veils the beauty of her face ...
Exquisite today,
This sport of love,
As Radha rides on Krishna.
Beads of sweat glisten on her face
Like pearls on the moon ..."

She was frothing on the bed, too happy to respond. Then she raised herself on one elbow.

"Not a single bead of sweat."

Elaborately contrite, he told her he would inform Vidyapati of his mistake.

"Who is this Vidyapati?"

"He was born in a village in northeast Bihar. My state. He was a Brahmin, who spent his life as a poet and scholar in service to Hindu kings who were threatened at that time by invading Muslim sultans."

She pretended to be disappointed. "I thought it was you."

He recited again:

"Listen, O lovely darling,
Cease your anger.
I promise by the golden pitchers of your breasts
And by your necklace-snake,
Which now I gather in my hands,
If ever I touch anyone but you
May your necklace bite me ..."

His eyes were closed. "The necklace was important to Vidyapati. It is the snake that bites the lover if he is unfaithful."

Against the sheets, starched bright and ironed white, she noticed the latency of his thigh and a bulging muscle on his shoulder. "And will you ever touch anyone but me?"

"Bind me in your arms, bruise me with your thighs ...
Lock me night and day in the prison of your heart."

He was lying on his back, his arms folded under his head. He smiled in a shy, sly manner. "He is famous for poems of passion and love, which he weaves around the story of Radha and Krishna."

She prods him with the real world, telling him of the long weekend in Mussoorie. He sits up, leaps from the bed, strides about the bungalow. She must grasp the significance of her first visit to the mountains, even if only to the foothills. It is a pilgrimage.

"The mountains are gods. The spiritual world of India is in the mountains. Here is Kailas, the holiest of the holy. Here is the sacred lake Mansarovar, the inspiration of artists. And Mahadeo, Dhaulagiri, Annapurna, Badrinath, Trishul and Nanda Devi."

The names roll from his tongue like marbles along a wooden tube. "Himavan is the god of the Himalayas and his daughter is Parvati, the wife of Shiva himself."

He is cheered by a clever thought. "And there is the Flood. You Christians have your story of Noah's Ark. Our Noah was Manu, who also had a boat, which was taken to safety in the Himalayas, drawn by a fish which was an incarnation of Vishnu."

He wiggles his head in pleasure at the parallel of their two worlds. "You see, we are all in the same boat."

He cannot resist an additional tick for his own culture. "Our story has a certain sophistication which is perhaps lacking in yours. In the boat with Manu were not representatives of the animals, as you have in Noah's Ark. We cover that aspect of evolution with the sacred fish and in the idea of reincarnation. No, in the boat with Manu were seven rishis, priestly scholars, who helped him to write a new order for India, our law, which is now inscribed on the mountain peaks."

He bows, as if to applause. "So our Noah was a kind of Moses also."

He stops, as if he has suddenly remembered what he had meant to say in the first place. "Remember the five elements." He takes her hands. "Earth, air, fire, water and space. Or man and woman, earth, sky and, in between, humankind. The five."

She repeats the words to humour him. Man. Woman. Earth, Sky. Humankind. The Five.

He is solemn, standing rigid, listening to her with his face alight, as if the words take on a magical quality when issuing from her lips. She cannot resist digging an elbow in his ribs.

"I know about man and woman."

4

THE TWO WOMEN CLAMBER DOWN the side of the road and brace at the mountain's edge, looking out over India. To the southeast is Nepal. To the northwest is Kashmir. Behind them are the mighty Himalayas. Before them is a great plain, stretching as far as the eye can see. They link arms around their waists.

"It makes you think, doesn't it?"

"About what?"

"Oh, life and the universe."

Annie listens to the woman, who is her mother's school friend. She tries to catch threads of her mother's voice in what the woman is saying but the years have treated them differently. The woman has become familiar with the rules of success, and she uses the clipped, cheerful voice that applies the rules to others. Her marriage has introduced her to foreign countries and cultures, strategies and tactics, margins and options. She has left behind the aches and pains of getting by. She is aware of the big picture, unlike Annie's mother, still bogged in the detail of survival, like the Indian masses struggling to get by on the great plain below.

When Annie looks down, she thinks of Gopala. On the drive to Mussoorie, she cried out in the car.

"Annie, are you alright?"

"Just a little carsick." An apologetic smile.

Pat stopped the car, blamed the bumpy, dusty, narrow roads, crowded with carts, cows and camels. A thermos of tea and some fresh scones, still warm, in a starched white napkin, revived them on the bank of a wide, slow-moving river. They sat in the shade of a loquat tree, after Pat used a croquet stick to clear the ground of orange coloured fruit and dark brown seeds.

Her host and hostess reclined in the back of the car for the rest of the journey, cool and thoughtful. She sat in the front, next to the turbanned driver.

"It's better in the front. You can see what's going on and you don't get that woozy feeling."

She saw him in village after dusty village, so crowded that the car was reduced to walking pace, in the main street, at roadside stalls under tarpaulin, in cement houses plunked unceremoniously in straw-coloured fields. When they left Dehra Dun and began to climb, winding slowly upwards, she saw him in a ragged forest in the foothills and by a rushing waterfall. When they arrived in Mussoorie, he was waiting for them in the mist on a mountain ledge. She saw him outside the dingy shophouses of Gandhi Chowk, on the English lawns of colonial retreats called something Castle, something Park, Court, Hall and Manor, on rickshaws on a promenade perched on rock along one side of the Mall, at the palaces, chateaus, hunting lodges, wolf's lairs and eagle's nests copied from Europe.

"When you look down there, you get some idea of the size of the problem," the woman says, sweeping the horizon with her disengaged arm.

"Which is?"

The woman hesitates, as if considering several possibilities, then announces her decision. "There's so many of them!"

"Not as many as in China."

The woman takes her arm away from Annie's waist and regards her young companion with feigned disapproval. "We mustn't spoil our day. Doesn't it feel good, just breathing in cool air?"

She breathes deeply and Annie feels obliged to follow her example. The two women stand on the edge of the road, with the earth falling away before them, and breathe deeply.

"The Chinese are different," the woman says. "So cheerful!" It is evident from the upward tilt of her nose that she is not prepared to say the same of Indians.

"It is crowded," Annie concedes, as they resume their walk. "But they know how to live like that, don't they?" She adds, intending to be helpful, "And, if living standards continue to improve, there will be a huge market."

"I used to think like that," the woman says. "But you give up after a while. You need evidence and it just isn't there. Just isn't there."

Annie wonders whether repeating yourself is a habit of foreigners who have lived in India long enough to have become anxious about being taken seriously.

"Just think, if they are successful." The woman has developed over time and some interesting diplomatic postings an aura of authority. She notices things and is able to recount with fair accuracy what has drifted her way at dinner parties and what her husband has told her in the safety of their marriage. "If all these billions have a house, a car and a fridge, there won't be room for anything else!" She directs her thinking at Annie. "Not just pollution, think of the disposal problem. The garbage!" Her thoughts expand. "And what about all that communication equipment, mobile phones, laptops, broadband and so on? They're mad about information technology."

She waves into space, as if it, too, is threatened.

"And good at it," Annie says. The woman needed to be brought back to earth. "How long have you and Pat been here?"

"This is our third year."

"Well, that's not long."

"Long enough."

The woman tosses her head, strides out valiantly on the gravel road. "If Patrick had his way, we would stay for another three. He loves it."

"I can understand why. It's a fascinating country."

"And what am I supposed to do?" Suddenly, in the middle of the road, the woman is distraught and angry, flinging out words. "You think it's a marvellous life, big house, parties, servants and everything? Well, let me tell you, it's ... it's ... not." She glares at Annie. "It's no bloody bowl of cherries, let me tell you."

Annie expects her to repeat "no bloody bowl of cherries" but instead she takes off at a stiff pace. After a brisk hundred metres, she resumes her relaxed and charming manner. "It gets my goat at times."

"I haven't heard that for ages." Annie flashes a smile of appreciation. "Gets my goat!"

"It must be Gardenvale coming out." The woman tosses Annie a secretive glance and then composes herself. "Actually, to be fair, it's been fun most of the time. We've had good times here."

"Better than Gardenvale," says Annie dutifully.

"Anything's better than Gardenvale."

The woman checks herself. It is one of the ground rules of their relationship that they do not talk about Annie's mother, or only so much as is necessary to avoid the conclusion that they do not wish to talk about her. Gardenvale, where Annie's mother still lives, is shorthand for what they have both left behind, but they avoid discussing what it is they have abandoned or the different routes they have taken to get away. They share an instinct that they have to keep moving.

"How's the project going? I know we keep asking and you keep answering, but I don't really have any idea what you're doing."

Annie had expected she would be asked to share confidences on long walks in the mountain air. Even without mentioning Gopala, it wasn't easy to explain the persistence of the Indian project in her life. It began in a school poetry class, discussing John Keats' "Ode on a Grecian Urn" ("O Attic shape ... silent form/ When old age shall this generation waste,/ Thou shalt remain ... 'Beauty is truth, truth beauty' – that is all/ Ye know on earth, and all ye need to know.") and William Wordsworth's "Tintern Abbey" ("And I have felt/ A presence that disturbs me with the joy/ Of elevated thoughts ... Whose dwelling is the light of setting suns,/ And the round ocean ... and in the mind of man.").

She wrote out in full the two poems and pasted them on the wall at the head of her bed. It had been her secret, tightly held, dark as a cave, light as the curl of a wave, dangerous and dazzling, more wondrous than the world of sex and emotion that all her friends thought was important. If she could connect the two worlds, attic shape and light of setting suns, she might discover how to live a life that was different from the one she was living and that everyone seemed to think was normal.

She decides she will be an archaeologist.

Brothers. Two to one. The youngest, she had always had them, like small fireworks displays, hot, noisy, dirty. They could not stand the peace and quiet of others, which they disrupted at will; if there was nothing else for them to do, they would wrestle each other. She grew up romping and chasing, the only way to keep up with them. If she tried to escape, they followed her, pushing and prodding her, poking their tongues at her, telling her she was a sissy. Suddenly, as if summoned, they would leave her and rush off to another part of the house. If they were quiet, she trembled with fear and excitement and tiptoed through passages and doorways looking for them.

She carried their spiked boots back from football matches. Their socks hung loose and they kicked their feet on the metal surface of the road as they slouched ahead, muddy and wounded. They so occupied her space and time that her mother and father were secondary characters. Like umpires, they tried to adjudicate and reprimand, occasionally extricating her from dangerous situations, as when she was tied to a tree stump alive with ants, but they were not part of the real world, never in the action. She hoped for a change as she grew older, but the situation became worse. Both parents were often at work and she was expected to do more in the kitchen.

Her father's temper was directed at her. He stood in the doorway glaring, a newspaper hanging from one hand, searching the room for the source of his anger, finding nothing, giving her a whack around the ears "for her trouble", a phrase whose meaning she never understood. Her mother dissolved into tears whenever Annie complained. She never protects Annie, never stands between her and the angry father. If Annie persists in crying, she goes to her room and closes the door.

"I am going to be an archaeologist."

"A what?"

She spells it out. "A-r-c-h-a-e-o-l-o-g-i-s-t."

When she tells them what archaeologists do, they think she must be mad, so she becomes more determined. She plots her courses at school so that she has the right prerequisites for university. From her early teens, she has this strangely precise ambition. While her friends talk vaguely about "being on television", she loves the television programs with teams digging up the past. They are like ordinary people, using picks and shovels, wearing working clothes, finding everyday things that people had used, not arty types talking their heads off at cocktail parties.

Her household clamours and bickers. Her parents are in league with the boys. She withdraws, applies herself to her studies and waits.

Eventually, it happens. One cold winter night, the school gym warmed by strip heaters on the walls, her name is called and she walks down the long passage between the rows of clapping parents and friends, up the steps to the platform and receives the prize. After that, she is allowed her peace and quiet. The boys cannot understand her need for it, but they accept that she requires it. No longer a sissy, she is now unfair and mean. Sometimes she is just rotten. She tries to play favourites but they are inseparable.

Later, when they leave home for jobs and games in a world outside, she learns to live in the house as a single person, almost as a stranger. An outsider in the family she had wanted to be part of, she does not care. She puts a bolt on the door, buys a clip-on lamp at a garage sale so that she can read properly in bed and gets rid of her mother's camphor balls. Once she decides to rely on herself, her life takes off. Everything comes together. Not a moment is wasted. No drugs, not much partying. Her friends are doing information technology, international business, computer science, but she stays on track. She drives her ambition like an engine on rails, forging ahead, only one way to go. The air rushes past, the landscape opens up. Nothing can stop her.

When the opportunity for a trip to India comes, she does not hesitate. Come on board, India!

"I've been meaning to talk to you about something," Annie says to the woman. "A personal matter."

"Of course." The woman stops in the roadway and turns warmly to her young companion.

"I don't know if you've noticed, but I've not known what to call you, how to address you. You were always Auntie Mim. But when I came here, I felt uncomfortable with that in front of everyone. It made me seem like a little girl, and it made you far too old. But you've never been called just Mim – and I'm certainly not going to call you Memsahib! I have no problem with Pat. I've always called him that ..."

"Call me Iris," the woman says.

"I wondered," Annie murmurs. She had noticed people calling the woman Iris, and wondered where the name came from. The name she had had when she wasn't Auntie Mim was Myrtle.

In the silence that follows, the pressure to explain themselves to each other is palpable. Whose turn it is remains in doubt, although the woman called Iris has her nose in the air and her eyes on the horizon.

"I do appreciate staying at the residence," says Annie humbly. She gains confidence, accelerating as the woman nods. "I know you've got the servants to run the place, but still, having a guest to think about all the time must be a drag. It's been a great help to me, staying somewhere pleasant. Very pleasant indeed. Not to mention the money side of things. So I do appreciate it." A helpful pause. "Iris."

The woman waves a slender hand, accepting the appreciation and at the same time brushing it aside.

"As for the project, well it's more interesting and demanding than I expected."

"Good!"

"Well, yes and no. I had thought it was something I could manage in a few weeks."

"Yes, but what is it?"

Iris has learned the knack of making a request sound like a demand. For no good reason, except perhaps self-preservation, and a sense that her India was not Iris's India, Annie hesitates. Normally, she enjoyed explaining the practicality of her work, but in India it was not the artefacts that mattered as much as the spirit flowing around them. She could have mentioned Jawaharlal Nehru's brilliant idea of Indian culture as a palimpsest, a piece of parchment from which writing was partially erased to make way for a new text. Indians lived in several centuries at the same time, the dreams of nomads and herders and priests shown in murals in caves all over the country giving way to the dreams of call centres in New Delhi and science and technology seminars in Bangalore. She could have spoken of new techniques of carbon dating or that characters similar to those on Indus River seals had been found on tablets excavated on Easter Island in the Pacific.

But when she thought of India, Gopala was there, his eyes playful above raised and pointed hands, and she was overwhelmed with guilt. Why, what was there to be guilty about? She remembered a phrase her mother used, tossed from twisted lips. They were having "a bit of a fling". That was all. She and Gopala were having a bit of a fling. It was a human experience. They were attracted to each other. You had to explore the world beyond your own little patch. A bit of adventure, or you'd be stuck in Gardenvale for the rest of your life. What was there to be guilty about?

Yet she felt guilty. And, underneath her protests, she knew why. It was not just "a bit of a fling" that could be managed within the rules that novels and films and gossip had established for public edification, to the satisfaction of twisted lips and knowing looks. And it was not just because of the pond and being a guest at the residence and pilfering petrol. She could deal with that, manage it or, if not, turn her back on it and walk away. It was something else, something she could neither walk away from nor explain to Iris.

The exquisite, excruciating, physical pleasure of making love.

Civilisation as Iris and her mother understood it did not include the experience of ecstasy. It was out there in the wilderness of wild youth and drug-induced fantasy, or in primitive or religious communities with strange customs, like painted bodies, tom-tom music and polygamy. By experiencing it, she had removed herself from the rules that governed their lives. Ecstasy was a rejection not just of decency, but reality – for her mother, humdrum domesticity, and for Iris, the discipline that elites imposed on themselves in order to govern the world.

She teased Iris. "I'm sure you don't want a dissertation. It's too nice a day for that, don't you think! Why don't we just breathe in this lovely cool air." And she strode out in front, swinging her arms and breathing deeply, until the moment passed. "Mustn't keep them waiting."

They are on their way to meet Pat at Killarney Cottage, the home of a maharaja and his wife.

They sit in a semicircle around a fire in the living room. Except for a horned trophy on one wall suggesting a past activity, the room is self-consciously idle. Books and magazines are scattered luxuriously. The obligatory television set and video rack are not visible. A large Saint Bernard sprawls on a Tibetan rug. The fire glows without spit and crackle.

The maharaja has survived Indian democracy by going into the real estate business. Hill stations like Mussoorie suffered in the years following independence, because the princely and warrior castes who had followed the British to the hills returned to the plains to find other roles. Real estate prices dropped and the maharaja bought. Then the new middle class of independent India rediscovered the hill stations and the maharaja sold.

"A wave of Indian wealth swept the old continent," he says grandly. "Now, another wave of Indian wealth is sweeping the old continent. Unfortunately, this time it is not sweeping the hill stations." He collapses into his jacket in amused resignation.

"They would rather holiday on the Riviera," says his wife. "Even London is not so popular these days."

"Deer-stalking in Hungary is popular," the maharaja confirms. "Some also like falconing in the Gulf states. Or looking for blood sucking vampires in Romania." He confronts an even more serious question. "And, of course, air-conditioning."

"Air-conditioning has made a tremendous difference," his wife affirms, as if to a jury of her peers. "And swimming pools."

"Swimming pools are extremely popular, especially with young people," the maharaja acknowledges. "Not just young people. A friend of ours has a swimming pool with a contraption at one end that creates waves. Very stimulating." He looks around the room, inviting comment. "Great fun." He is not opposed to progress. "Globalisation. The Internet. That sort of thing." But air-conditioning and swimming pools cannot compare with the pure air of Mussoorie.

A view of almost 360 degrees. That is the perspective of a ruined house high on a hill at Jaberkhet, empty for so long that no one can now recall anyone having lived in it. The garden is so overgrown that it is impossible to know where it begins or ends, the maharaja mentions, as if that might be an inducement to purchase, and the lawns have developed a tough grass that is self-sustaining, able to survive the snow. There is room in the tangled garden for a tennis court and croquet lawn but some might think the garden is itself an attraction.

"Rambling roses," says the maharani. Dissatisfied in an indefinable way, she does her best to extract satisfaction from the ruined house. "Some people say it's haunted." Underneath were found oven trays, as for scones, with smaller indentations, as for sweets.

"Boiled lollies," says the maharani.

The maharaja has the necessary papers, if anyone is interested in buying, but the owner's identity is a mystery. "I've never had a contract of sale with a ghost before," he says cheerfully.

A lull in the conversation follows of such length that the maharani is forced back on what is evidently her favourite topic. "There's a limit to the number of times you can play 'Ah, Sweet Mystery of Life, I've Found Thee' on the piano," she announces. "Especially if the piano needs tuning."

"I thought that had been arranged."

The maharani adopts an injured look. "You think lots of things have been arranged."

He leans over to pat her hand. "Bubbles." He pats her hand again, looking at their guests. "She used to be bubbly."

She primps at Bubbles and dislikes being called the maharani, although what she dislikes most of all is the way the men in Mussoorie seem always to be wrapped in scarves or blankets. There are three ways to wear a scarf: wrapped around the forehead like a sweatband, wrapped from the back of the head to the nose, under which it is tied, covering the mouth, and wrapped under the chin and tied on top of the head, as though suffering from the mumps. She is tired of all of them. She hitches her sari over her shoulder when she is agitated, which she does now. "You would think they might try to look a little less disreputable."

Her dark good looks have become with age even more forceful, with her white hair and pale skin and the decline of any desire to be pleasing. She has settled into a commentary on life that notices practicalities near at hand, is suspicious of heights and depths and is without affection for foothills. The maharaja has aged differently, becoming thoughtful as earthly prizes recede, at peace with the world, but whether because he has come to terms with its shortcomings or his own remains untested. He is bald, with a shiny head. His handlebar moustache has waxed ends. He is dressed in twill trousers and a tweed jacket, like a European gentleman, but he is wearing running shoes with heavily built-up soles, creating an ungainly conclusion to his trimly trousered legs.

Annie is lost in the decomposition of her surroundings. She feels she has come to the wrong house by mistake but cannot find an excuse, or summon up the confidence, to leave. She grits her teeth, leans forward in her chair and, under a perpetual frown, painfully smiles as the afternoon rings with false laughter. When tea arrives, she is numbed by the prospect of an extended stay, terrified that out of courtesy and boredom attention will turn to her and she will be required to explain her project to an audience even less interested than Pat and Iris and, in their innocence, more dangerous.

Pat and Iris rise to the occasion. They had persuaded Annie that the pair were a popular couple who knew everyone and everything in Mussoorie and they realise that it is up to them to make the occasion tolerable. They tut and exclaim, oh and really, you don't say, well I never, fancy that, you can never tell, pout and smile as if they have been scripted. The afternoon wobbles and wanders on, powered by tittle-tattle, rising and falling on wafts of forced labour, ending with a doorway crescendo in which the couples embrace and promise not to allow time to prevent a renewal of the happy occasion.

They walk home in mauve twilight.

"Look!" says Pat, pointing. "There's a lyre tree. They say they're unique to Mussoorie."

They admire a thinly covered tree, with branches of a shape that gives it its name.

"Not the only thing unique to Mussoorie." Iris laughs heartily at her own quip and Annie joins her.

"It was hard work," admits Pat. "You have to admire them, though."

"Why admire?" Iris sides with Annie. "Poor thing. Bored out of her wits."

"Oh, well." Pat is not sure why the maharaja and the maharani should be admired. "Sticking it out, I suppose."

"Hanging on. What's admirable about that?"

"Well, there's a bit of character in what they're doing. A kind of loyalty. Better than Monte Carlo or deer hunting in Hungary. Or falconing, for God's sake."

"Why?" asks Iris. She has the honesty of the newly converted.

Pat does not know, or prefers not to say, so remains silent. He likes conversations in which people agree with each other, even when they are not sure what is being said. It is more civilised than arguing about everything in public.

"Mussoorie's probably all they can afford," says Iris.

"That's a bit unkind."

"Well, my instinct is that she would rather be somewhere else, if she had the choice."

Pat keeps his thoughts to himself. It is not wise to contest the reliability of Iris's instincts.

Annie has stopped listening. She is watching mist settle on red-roofed buildings on a spur off the main road, overlooking the valley. She is thinking that even here, poised between heaven and earth, reality gets in the way. Real reality, the humdrum sort. No Attic shape nor silent Form. No dwelling of Light, in the mind or anywhere else. Just Killarney Cottage, with a couple of relics in it. Ordinary life gets you in the end.

She goes outside at night to look at the stars, to smell the trees and to wonder about the void that stretches below. She cries out when she sees the stars. They are so close they hover, palpitating over her head. If she jumps, she will surely touch them, so she jumps, twice, three times, stretching one hand into the night. Taking hold of herself, she stands still and closes her eyes. She catches a whiff of wet earth, roots and bark. A lacing of leaves. She had seen the trees during her walk. Deodars, covered with wisps of moss. Big, shapely cypress, dark green. Cedar. Oak. She can smell the rank undergrowth of rhododendron and wild cherry, with airs of daphne and jasmine.

She opens her eyes and, leaning over the balcony, looks out over India. The vast habitation that she knows is there shows up as blank darkness, a crater of bottomless black. The Five! Man and woman, sky and earth and him in between, somewhere down there with all the rest of humankind, in the middle of nothingness. She tries to see him in her mind, to think about him. She grips the rails to concentrate and closes her eyes again. Nothing happens.

"Please, God," she whispers. She corrects herself. "Hamivan." She shouts into the sweet, dank air. "Anyone!" She whispers "please" again and again. The stars twinkle crisply above her head. The wet earth smells rise in waves around her. His image does not appear. She entreats, a croak now in her voice. Nothing. The black void of India beneath her is empty and motionless.

She gives up and goes inside, so flat and desolate that they ask if she is alright. She says she has had an unusually strenuous day and would like to go to bed early. In bed, warm and tearful, she sees him. He is striding about the compound, eyes glinting, body coiled to spring. He is lying on the big teak bed, black on white on brown. He is scribbling his poems at the little desk by the window. She drifts off to sleep, crushing a pillow in her arms.

5

EACH DAY OF HER ABSENCE, Gopala consulted an Australian calendar hanging over the big teak bed. Under a group picture of blond surf-riders, posed like medieval knights in their wetsuits with boards like shields under their arms, he fixed his eye on the number corresponding to the day. He concentrated on it, piercing it with his imagination, seeing her. She walked, and he watched every ripple of her body, especially how her legs pushed against her skirt. She ate and he watched the movement of her lips, a glimpse of her teeth as she smiled and talked. She leaned towards him and he saw the flesh of her neck and the hint of her breasts. She smoked and he saw the blue fume forming in the air. He wished she would stop smoking.

Each day as he went about his work in the compound, he imagined what she would be doing. Foreigners always went walking in Mussoorie, along the Mall or on Camel's Back Road, striding on the gravel roads through the hills, marvelling at the snow-capped mountains at their back and the vast plain of India beneath them. Would she walk in the morning or the afternoon? It would depend on the weather, but at this time of the year it was usually fine. If rain did threaten, it was in the afternoon, when the heat from the plains had had time to rise. On the other hand, the sky was almost always deceptively clear. The rain happened so suddenly that you were given no warning, like an accumulation of cloud, so that you might set out for a walk with a clear sky and be caught in a downpour. On balance, she was probably a morning walker. Her host and hostess were.

So he had her strolling, striding rather, each morning around the hills of Mussoorie, probably with them, although she was in many ways a solitary, independent person. Very independent. So sometimes she would be alone. He alternated the days. On the first day, the three of them. On the second day, the two women. On the third day ... Was it possible that she would walk only with the man? He saw them together. Their eyes swivelled at each other as they strode side by side along the gravel road. They stopped, turned together and stood, admiring the view. He saw the man bending solicitously over her. He saw him touch her arm. He saw her touch his shoulder!

Gopala went grimly about his work. He did not trust the man. He tried too hard to be liked, which was not a good sign. It meant he was weak, needed something, like the soft arms of a woman. Especially a woman who owed him something, like weeks of rent. It was difficult for the man to do anything in the residence, because everyone was watching. But in Mussoorie, on a lonely road, with no one around? Who could tell what might happen? Gopala was sure, absolutely certain, that the man desired her. Why else did he put up with her staying at the residence all this time? And how much did he know about what went on in the bungalow? Gleeson had his spies and the residence staff was full of social climbers. What if he blackmailed her? Alright, you can stay in the house, but on one condition!

He saw the man walking with her on a mountain road. They strode along briskly, glancing at each other, then stopped, breathed deeply together and admired the view. He saw the man leading her by the hand, pulling her really, down the side of the road into a clump of bushes. She was resisting, but what could she do? Anyway, she was only half-resisting. Gopala shuddered as the man thrust his face against hers and searched for her lips. She was not really resisting. Of course she wasn't. Think of the way she came to him in the moonlight at the bottom of the garden. She made it clear what she wanted. He would never have dared to make a move. You not only can lose your job, you can finish up in gaol for that sort of thing. But she wanted it, she was asking for it. She touched him ... there! Well, almost. He was sure of it.

If she would do this for him, someone she could not even see properly in the dark, she would do it twice as readily for a man from her own country, who had known her for ages, who had power over her and who desired her madly. And was a successful man of the world, used to making quick decisions.

Look at her afterwards, coming to the bungalow. She was hungry for it.

Gopala rushed out of his tiny office, which was an old sentry box. He strode through the garden down to the pond. He stood there with his eyes closed, reliving the night they met, forcing the scenes from Mussoorie out of his mind.

When they returned, holiday-makers tumbling out of the car with the servants lined up in front of the residence, she expected him to be lurking cleverly nearby. The servants took the luggage and offered soothing drinks after the long drive. Usually, someone from security would be around when the master returned, but not this time. As soon as she could, she bicycled to the bungalow, but he was not there. The servant thought he was at work.

She found him by the petrol pump. His eagerness had gone. His body was straight, not coiled and slippery, and withdrawn, like his watchful eyes. When she approached, with a bit of a smile and a small swing of her hips, he turned his back and walked to the other side of the pump. She pursued him.

"What mischief have you been up to while I've been away?"

She addressed her remarks to two mechanics as well, but they grinned and melted away, leaving the lovers facing each other.

"I had a nice time in the mountains. Fresh air, walks, that kind of thing." She dropped her voice. "And I did not forget the Five."

He neither smiled nor flinched. He was a soldier on parade being inspected by a visiting dignitary.

"Did you manage in my absence?" she asked engagingly.

"Yes, memsahib." He was obsequious, laying it on with a trowel.

Challenged, she moved close to him. He withheld himself physically as if her presence, although unavoidable, was distasteful. On the pebbled floor her toes crept from her sandals to the tips of his shining shoes. She touched his arm lightly. Her hair fell over her face and she playfully tossed it back.

"I never stopped thinking of you," she whispered.

"Good afternoon, memsahib."

He turned on his heel and marched away, his shoulders square, his arms swinging manfully.

She had agreed, on the drive back from Mussoorie, to accompany Pat and Iris to a dinner party that evening. As she dressed, she devised a scheme in which she would become ill and be brought home. But she could not ride the bicycle at night: it had no lights. Was it safe to ask the driver to take her to the bungalow? No, it was not. She would have to get a taxi. But the servants would know if she ordered a taxi from the residence. How would she explain her sudden departure into the night in a taxi when she had returned home early from the dinner party because she was unwell? She could say that she felt better and was returning to the party, then redirect the taxi driver en route. It was possible.

"Ready, Annie?"

They were waiting at the door for her. She left with her plan of escape half formed.

In the car, Iris's perfume and Pat's shiny, dinner-party look confirmed her irritation: she was not going to enjoy herself. She should never have agreed, but they were so good to her and they had pressed her, as if they couldn't themselves bear to go unless she came with them, or that it was a social tribulation only her company could make tolerable. Yet they were prepared to enjoy themselves, primed professionally for a good time, and she resented unreasonably their deception, their charm and calculated sociability. As they chirped about the people she was going to meet, she set her mind on her escape plan.

The host and hostess were framed in the entrance hall of their luxurious house like a pair of dancers, holding hands, pirouetting on their toes. The guests were a medley of foreigners, rich Indians and Bollywood hopefuls, all of whom seemed to know each other; she was the only person who needed to be introduced. Each person paused over each introduction as if it were a rite of passage. The women held her hand while they asked her questions about her visit to India; the men looked lengthily into her eyes and inquired about her favoured form of entertainment. She could not stand them! She began to feel faint.

She signalled to Iris and in the bathroom explained that she was not feeling well.

"What is it, dear?" Iris's smile was an uneasy mix of concern and irritation.

"It's my time of the month, I think." Annie had decided on this in the car. "I shouldn't have come, but ... you were really insistent, so kind in pressing me, that I felt I had to respond." She thought this worked quite well.

"Have a glass of water. What about an aspirin? Perhaps you'll be alright if you sit quietly for a moment?"

"I'd rather just slip away, before we sit down. It will be much worse if I have to leave in the middle of dinner. I'm sorry, Iris, to be a nuisance, but would you please explain now to our hostess, so that she can rearrange the seating, and would you kindly get the car to take me back to the residence."

By using all the phrases Iris used, she made her request sound like an order.

"I'll sit quietly here and wait," she said finally. And sat quietly, waiting.

It all happened as she had decreed, except that she was so pleased with herself on the drive home that she forgot to behave as if she were indisposed. She chatted to the driver and when they turned into the circular driveway she opened the car door before they had arrived at the front of the residence, jumping out with cheerful thanks and letting herself inside the house. When a servant appeared, she smiled wanly and explained she was going to her room to rest. She flung herself on her bed and glared at the ceiling.

Suddenly the lights went out, a hazard in power-hungry India. It would take a minute or two of darkness and a distant whirring sound before the compound generator switched on. She stood at the window and watched torches slicing the dark. Raised voices contended. She could make out lumbering shapes.

This was her chance to make a break, while the compound was preoccupied and road traffic was light. She would use a torch, strapped with tape to the handlebars. Every room had a torch for emergencies. She found hers, switched it on; it worked. There was tape in the bathroom. Before the generator groaned and whirred and brought light again to the big house, she was down the stairs and out the side door to the porch where she parked the bicycle. A few swift circles of tape bound the torch to the left handlebar (the right one carried the handbrake). A click of the switch and it was on –and she was off, into the wide, dark street.

She knew the route so well that even in the darkness she had no trouble finding her way. There were few cars. Bicycles were the main danger, many without lights. Their white-shirted riders flew at her out of the night like ghosts. At last she could see the library and speeded to reach the bungalow. She could see a glimmer of light through a window. Still panting, she approached the door, tapped and waited, her heart pounding.

He opened the door with one hand, holding a candle in the other.

She stepped quickly towards him. Even while he still held the candle, she put her arms around his neck. She pushed herself against him, while he searched for a place to stand the candle. Then his arms were free and he crushed her to his black-statue body. He took her in one long swoop to the big teak bed and threw himself on her, holding her arms out from her body high and straight, pushing his full weight on her, whimpering with little cries of anguish and delight.

"Oh!" she cried unexpectedly and wriggled herself free. She scrambled from the bed and stumbled in candlelight to the door, leaving him floundering, his face, buried in bedclothes, half-turned in search of her. Then she was back, throwing off her party dress, easing herself under him with an apologetic smile.

"I forgot to switch off the torch."

He heard nothing. He was lost in her, emitting his little cries, contracting and extending every muscle in his potent body.

This was the night she flew among the clouds. Nothing could stop her, not even the hard, high ridge. "My horse! My horse!" The twinges of guilt she had felt in the mountains vanished. She took off, soared; it was like one of those near-death experiences, she imagined, when you are drawn to dazzling light but remain immersed in your body. She was floating on clouds, which she had wanted to do since she was a little girl, and experiencing at the same time the most excruciatingly beautiful bodily sensations she had ever known. His hard, strong body was everywhere, but he was no longer a furious elephant. He was as lithe and sure-footed, as tireless and powerful, as a leopard.

They held each other so fiercely at times that they were like a single body, a rod of steel, immobile, fused with tension, unable to move, absorbing each other. Then she felt his muscles subside, his body unravel. One of his hands moved. A toe touched the sole of one of her feet, his shoulders softened, his neck craned and his face came to rest against hers. He hunched suddenly and his lips travelled down her body, her breasts, one and then the other, her inner thighs, behind her knees, the calves of her legs, each of her toes, which he rolled in his wet mouth like lollies. Annie lay still, unable to move, fizzing and frothing, gurgling with the pleasure of being handled like a precious treasure.

Later, as they lay together on the big teak bed, he murmured in her ear.

"Your secret is out, why are you so shy?
His forces of love
The god has roused in you.
Your thighs tremble.
The golden skin of your breasts
Is scarlet from his nails
Yet still you try to hide them."

She smiled, and stroked his hair while she told him about Mussoorie.
"And on the third day?"
"Oh dear," she said, trying to remember. "All the days run into one."
"Did you walk on Camel's Back Road with Mr Shard?"
"With Pat? No, with Iris."
"He is interested in you."
"Pat! Come off it."
"Of course he is. He's behind all this investigation into the petrol supplies. He wants to get rid of me so that he can have you."

She burst into laughter. "Poppycock!"
"Not poppy. His." He shook with grim laughter. But his crudity took her by surprise and she became indignant. "He hasn't said a word to me about the petrol, or you or anything else. And his behaviour is absolutely ..." She sought a word which would convey her sense of the irreproachable quality of Pat. "... impeccable."

Gopala was lying with his head resting on crossed arms, his profile stern, his eyes, when he turned them slowly in her direction, without their marbled softness, hard and beady. "You owe him money."
"I do not."
"You're staying in his house."

"I'm an old family friend!"

Gopala was silent but unsatisfied.

"You're jealous." She remembered a refrain from schooldays. "Jelly, jelly jealous!"

She poked him in the ribs, pushing and pummelling until something like a smile appeared.

"Is Australia more free than India?" he asked, as if he had suddenly just thought of it.

"Free?" She flicked through intellectual options, but played safe. "It's more expensive."

"Of course. It is a developed country."

"Developed?" She shrugged her shoulders.

"I mean free from ..." Gopala gestured. "Free to ..."

"Voting is compulsory."

He nodded. "A civic duty, like paying taxes. We should have compulsory voting here. It would cut down the graft at election time."

She waited, not in the mood for a lesson in civics.

"Society is more open?" he asked hopefully. "Your culture is more relaxed."

"Relaxed?" Annie hesitated. "India is relaxing."

"For a visitor, but if you lived here you would find it not relaxing. A strong culture limits your freedom. In Australia you don't have lots of rules about personal behaviour, things like that?"

"You're joking. The place is riddled with rules! Someone's always wagging a finger at you."

"Really!" He showed his surprise by looking directly into her eyes. "It is not a permissive society?"

"Permissive?" She considered the word carefully and found its implications unsatisfactory. "Not by a long shot. They're at you night and day."

Gopala listened carefully with his swimming pool face. "But your public transport is very good? Trains and buses."

"Shocking. Public transport in Australia is the pits!"

"But better than here?"

She looked at Gopala as if he were lacking in some simple and essential ingredient of common sense. "Of course."

Satisfied but subdued, he sought more tractable terrain. "Australian men are healthy?"

"God, no."

He could not tell whether she was joking. "They are unhealthy? But there is a high living standard. Income per capita."

"They're slobs. Or fitness fanatics." Not like Gopala. "My horse!" she cried.

Gopala was not amused. He frowned and lifted his nose. "Why do you say 'My horse, my horse'?" and while she struggled to respond, "Sometimes you call me 'Ducky'. Is that a duck?" He was pretending to be merely curious, but disapproval lurked in a pouted smile.

"You started it, furious elephant."

"That was Vidya. Vidya's poems are like a screen, to keep real life away. Real life is families and work and the cost of everything."

"Is that what your poems are about?"

Gopala's eyes clouded with the impossible task of saying what his poems were about. His head swayed indecisively. Annie did not care. Poetry conned people into thinking that being sensitive was important, when the real thing was down at ground level, doing what everyone else was doing, or doing what everyone says you shouldn't be doing. Not much sensitivity down there. So she explained instead that she thought of him as a sure-footed leopard. Perhaps leopards were higher in the reincarnation scale than horses and ducks.

Gopala was fixed on something else. "It is sacred, what we are doing together." When he was serious, his face lost its shine, withdrew.

"It's only sex." The words escaped from her, like "having a fling".

He would not be deflected. Sex should not be treated lightly. It was up there with the spaciousness of the setting sun and Indian civilisation. And more.

"It is the most beautiful thing in the world."

"Yes, but ... Well, it's fun, too, isn't it?"

"Fun?"

Gopala was again upright. He remained silent for a long time. She wondered what fun meant to him. She glanced at his impassive face. She searched for another word, but in her languid state could not find one. He stirred, as if he had found the key to his thoughts.

"In a poor country like India, joy is possible, but fun is not."

His eyes narrowed as he struggled with the notion of India's poverty. She sometimes thought at these moments that he might break off suddenly and declare himself to be a revolutionary. "I have heard ..." he said. She had learned this meant something he had picked up at work. "Is it true that you have a national holiday in Australia on the day of a horse race?" He was having trouble keeping his face in order.

"Yes." Let him deal with it.

"And it is always on a Tuesday, so people can take the Monday off as well." He was wide-eyed with astonishment or (was it?) admiration. "You have a four-day weekend!"

"Yes." When they dug up Melbourne in a thousand years the evidence would be conclusive.

But what was he getting at? She wondered if he was no longer her noble statue but just another Indian angling for a working visa in Australia, as her mother and Iris would say.

"Of course, in India we believe in the deferred good."

Annie relaxed. He had that look on his face.

"Satisfaction postponed is pleasure prolonged."

He was right, of course. He could beat the Kenyans at long distance. "And Indian women?"

"Ah!" Delighted with her interjection, Gopala turned on her his sweet, vulnerable smile. "In the perfect union between man and woman, the mind and the body are in harmony." He was suddenly in her arms, her little boy, nestling. She rocked him like a baby. "There, there."

"I cannot bear the thought of another man with you," he mumbled. He burrowed in the bedclothes, his eyes closed.

6

IRIS WAS UPSET. FOR THE first time since Annie had come to live at the residence, she did not inquire cheerfully at breakfast how her guest had slept. She managed no more than a curt "good morning", got up from the table before Annie had finished and, without excusing herself, left for some undisclosed business in an unspecified place. However, Pat wanted to talk.

"You're a clever girl," he said, looking over his glasses at her as he glanced through a morning newspaper.

"Clever?"

"Yes, clever." He put down the newspaper. "That was really boring, last night."

"Oh, that." She feigned nonchalance. "Nature must be allowed to take its course."

"What's that supposed to mean?" Pat's blue eyes could be open to the world, or pinpointed as now.

"I thought Iris would have told you."

"She didn't say anything. Though she's obviously grumpy."

"I had a little visitor."

"Called who or what?"

He seemed determined to bear down on her, force her into the open, appraise her, make some kind of judgment.

"Oh, Pat!"

She blushed and looked away. Pat and Iris did not have children, so there had never been interlocutors of her age; they were like her parents, detached from Gardenvale. He continued to watch her, as if mildly annoyed with her. He yawned. Perhaps he was just tired. She ate her breakfast, but was overcome by a trivial sensitivity to the sound of toast crunching in her mouth. She tried to muffle the sound by moving her jaws slowly, but in the spans of silence it reverberated in her head even more loudly. She raised the cup of coffee to her lips to soak the toast, and sipped noisily.

She could not work out what was going on behind Pat's eyes. Usually, he was out there in the world, managing important matters, a public official as much as a family friend. He had once described to her the difference between strategies and tactics. He was convinced that understanding the difference, and acting within each category, not confusing one with the other, was the key to managing the challenges of life. He had also said that professional women were "slowly learning" that successful management was decision-making, not networking. These were the only fruits of his experience he offered her. Otherwise, he liked to chat about amusing events on the "daily grind". He was kind to her and helpful; his duty was to see that she enjoyed herself and did not get into trouble. And that was that. So why was he looking at her so intently with mirthless blue eyes?

"I think it's time you and I had a talk, don't you, young lady?"

Annie stopped her slow and careful munching of toast and swallowed. "About?"

"Oh, life and the universe, that sort of thing."

Annie glanced at her watch. Did he mean the same as Iris did, when they stood together looking down on the teeming plain? "Do you mean now?"

"No time like the present. Or have you got something on?"

"No, it's fine with me. But you are so busy in the mornings."

Pat brushed this aside by folding the paper and placing it neatly on the breakfast table. "Not today." He hunched up his shoulders and leaned forward, as if making a presentation. "Look, Iris asked me to speak to you. She didn't want to do it herself. I don't know why. She's got herself into a mood over last night. Anyway, the point is this ..."

He paused, dropping his eyes for the first time from their intense scrutiny. She could feel her heart beating faster.

"By the way, have you got your mobile with you? No? Alright. The point is this ... You've got to stop seeing this fellow."

Annie blushed all over her body. Pat leaned back, relieved, cheerful. "The tongues are wagging. After you left the party last night, Iris was given an earful, apparently."

"A fearful earful."

"It's no laughing matter, Annie. You don't seem to appreciate what sort of fellow, your ... this man is."

Pat's eyes twinkled, as if he enjoyed the situation he was about to describe. "You know, of course, that he's in trouble on the compound. Gleeson has explained all that to you. He's been using your name and the authority of the residence to make a bit on the side. In the normal way, he'd have been given his pay and bundled out the door, but because you backed up his story, Gleeson's been put in an awkward position."

"Good."

Pat observed Annie thoughtfully.

"We know how to handle this kind of problem in-house, so I didn't speak to you about it immediately. But when it gets out and around to such an extent that Iris is put on the spot at a dinner party, I take a different view."

Annie gathered her wits as Pat presented the case against her. She knew the strength of it even before he spoke; she felt it even more keenly than he did. She was pretending to be working on her project, while she was actually neglecting it while she bounced around on the big teak bed. And Pat was absolutely correct. Gopala had no right to use her name and the authority of the residence. Nevertheless.

She felt like a schoolteacher getting the logic right in an argument for proper behaviour outside of class, or like a preacher preparing the ground for a sermon on the supernatural origin of human existence. When your case was weak, you needed a good defence. Nevertheless, she would not give up the right to see Gopala as she wished. On or off the big teak bed. She would not allow Pat and Iris, nor the surrogate authority of the residence, the compound and the cockatoos (not to mention the unmentionable Gleeson) to tell her how she should live her life. It was her human right to decide with whom she was intimate. End of statement from the dock, your worship.

"I'm really sorry, Pat, to have caused you and Iris any trouble. You have been very kind to me and I've enjoyed being here with you. It never occurred to me that my private life would become an issue for you. Obviously, I must leave the residence. I'll move out this morning."

But that was not what Pat was suggesting. On the contrary, he and Iris wanted her to stay. Indeed, they enjoyed having her. That's what family friends were for, weren't they? No, the problem was the gossip. You can't get away with this sort of thing in India. The servants knew everything. Some of them were in league with ... well, police and intelligence, that sort of thing. The whole country was undergoing a change. The Nehru family had kept things under control, caste and that sort of thing, but now ... Muslims and terrorists, Maoists, Naxalites, some people thought the place was breaking up. And there was her work. The residence was a good base to work from – comfortable, all the facilities and services, close to everything. No, what he was suggesting was that she should continue to stay at the residence and that she should continue her interesting research, but ...

"You stop seeing ... this man." Without enthusiasm, Pat added, "In this way."

He said that Gopala would not be sacked. He could keep his job on the compound, although he had blotted his copybook and couldn't expect promotion. There was nothing to stop her speaking to him in a normal way, if they happened to meet in the course of his duties, but ...

"I've got to stop visiting his bungalow?"

"Well, yes." Pat became thoughtful, as if reluctant to accept so precise an injunction. "Look, you're an adult." He peered into a labyrinth of possibilities. "There are ways ..."

"I won't."

Pat had an ear for precision. Experience had made him careful. "You won't visit?"

"I won't stop."

Her crude defiance struck him like a light blow to the face. He was not accustomed to being opposed directly. She could see it had probably been years since anyone had been so openly uncooperative. She felt sorry for him.

"I know you are trying to do the best for me," she said, touching his hand. "But I can't allow anyone to tell me what I should or should not do in my private life. If I am embarrassing you, and especially Iris, which apparently is the case, I am willing, indeed anxious, to remove that embarrassment by making plain there is no complicity on your part. But that is as far as I can go. You must see that. Don't you?"

She was appealing to him as one responsible human being to another, but he seemed to be gripped by considerations that had escaped her notice. Not only had the dam burst, but also the cat was out of the bag, also among the pigeons, the milk was spilt, the deed was done, the bird had flown, the die was cast.

"You've stepped over the traces, young lady." He persisted, with the energy of conviction. "What do you see in him? He's not your sort of person."

"What do you mean?" She kept her voice level, even-tempered.

"Well, I'd be surprised if you had a great deal in common." Pat was still in negotiation mode, edging towards middle ground.

Annie became both angry with him and sorry for him, an explosive combination. She maintained an icy calm.

"Do you mean he's beneath me, because he's a guard on the compound and because he's black?"

"He is quite dark," Pat murmured reflectively.

"He's as black as the ace of spades." Her words pierced the cosy comfort of the breakfast room. "And, I can tell you, he's an ace in more than colour. He can trump anyone around here." She spared Pat, waving at the house, the compound, beyond. "And he's not just a guard, if that's what bothers you. He's a poet ... who knows more about what's going on in this country than all the residences and compounds and dinner parties put together."

It was inevitable that she should now stand. Whether she would sweep herself from the room was still in question.

"If he were one of your chattering cockatoos, would it be alright?" She flounced her hips. "Is that what you are saying?"

Pat was a sensible man, a manager, sufficiently experienced in the ways of men and women to know that it was sometimes prudent to step back. He acknowledged defeat.

"Well, if your mind is made up," he said, also standing, "that's the way it has to be. But be careful. And let's keep in touch."

They nodded to each other, as if sealing an understanding, and walked out of the breakfast room together. Within half an hour, she had also walked out of the residence. While she waited for a taxi the servants had summoned, she scribbled a note of thanks to Iris on a pad in the entrance hall.

She went straight to the bungalow. Anger and defiance combined with the practical need to find somewhere to live. If he were not there, she would leave her luggage and go to the library. The servant informed her that he had left for work. She gave the servant her things and departed on foot for the library.

It was one of those days when you could actually feel the air heating up. She had always been so excited when she was riding through this area that she had not noticed how bleak and gritty it was. Street trees were few and undernourished. Garden shrubs were filmed with dust. Houses, small in large allotments, looked unattended, even unwanted. On a big building that was a school, a ceramic mural, once glazed, had lost its colour and shine. On a roundabout, however, a Moghul dome was still a startling blue.

She strode determinedly, sometimes on the uneven road, sometimes on the broken footpath, sometimes across semi-vacant allotments cluttered with advertising billboards. Geese wandered across her path. A horn blared and a taxi stopped. A hand on a long, thin arm waved at her. In the shadow of the driver's compartment, a young, bearded face crowned with an orange turban entreated her with words she could not understand.

The residence had been a cocoon. Now she had to make the kind of practical decisions she had been told were so difficult in India, such as anything to do with transport. The buses were too rickety and crowded even to consider. If you didn't have a bicycle or a motor scooter, your choice was auto-rickshaw or taxi. The taxis were ramshackle and driven by men who sometimes behaved like guerrillas from a nearby battlefield. Her first ride in a taxi in India had taken her across a moon-face of landscape and deposited her at the wrong place. The yellow and black rickshaws were much cheaper than the taxis but physically vulnerable to other forms of traffic, especially lumbering buses and careening trucks. They were supposed to have two side mirrors, but often had only one, covered with grey mould spots. The leather seats were usually ripped. The meters were almost always "broken", so you had to barter for a price before the journey began. However, she liked the shrines some drivers erected below the windscreen: pictures of gods or glamorous women, always with garlands of flowers.

She could see the library and waved the taxi away. If she stayed at the bungalow, she could walk to the library, but she would need a bicycle for shopping.

Reassured by the library's familiar surroundings, she ordered books she had long intended to read. The staff kept an eye on her and tried to anticipate her wishes. The counter girl with the glossy hair brought her a cup of tea and a biscuit precisely at eleven o'clock. The reading room was not air-conditioned, but the air was pleasantly cool, stirred by low-slung fans that droned quietly. She stopped working and listened to the fans. The rhythm told her "don't give up ... keep on going". Work was important. So was knowledge. Keep at it. She wondered if the library had its own generator.

The counter girl said there was "a sort of" coffee shop in the building, "a bit like" a canteen. She never ate there. She brought her own lunch, indicating under the counter a collection of seemingly interoperable pots bound together by bureaucracy's pink tape. "We're allowed to use the tape," she explained quickly.

Click! The Indian way. Annie saw Gopala reclining on the big teak bed. A few pannikins of petrol here, a bit of tape there – and the mighty river of life rolled down to the sea.

The girl was now in the grip of a nervous disorder, twisting on her heels, looking shyly away, then back to watch Annie's face. She spoke so fast Annie had trouble catching what she was saying. "We could share, if you like curry, it's not very hot." She added, as if required to do so by law: "It's vegetarian."

They sat together under a porch covered with a sweet-smelling vine, a popular spot for lunch. Most of the staff were women, but two were men. Some of the young women came up to Annie, touched her hair, fingered the texture of her blouse. They said nothing, waiting to overhear what others said. Some watched from a distance. The men talked to each other, but found it difficult to keep their eyes from Annie.

The girl behaved as if she were personally responsible for Annie's welfare. When it was time to return to work, she escorted Annie back to her table, pulled out her chair and when she was ready to be seated, pushed it back. Annie wondered what she was expected to do in return.

Indian civility was puzzling. The country was pulsing with raw life, incontinent and even dangerous. Yet a core of restraint and deference remained in personal relations. She was no visiting foreign dignitary, merely an unknown Australian researcher intent on discovering whether Wordsworth had got it right about India as Keats had got it right about Greece. You would expect at a library respect for scholarship, but she wondered if they secretly shared the objective of her inquiry.

She was waiting for him when he arrived at the bungalow. She stood up as he entered, standing still and silent as he wrestled with surprise and confusion.

"I did not see the bicycle."

"It's not there. I came by taxi." She indicated her luggage. "I've come to stay." Laughing nervously. "If you'll have me."

He approached her slowly, his eyes fixed on hers. He pursed his lips. "Stay here?"

"Yes. Right in one." Her cheeks were flushed.

"Is that wise?"

"Probably not. But I got thrown out, so I didn't have much choice, did I? Well, not exactly thrown out. Let's say it was made difficult for me to stay. Is that being thrown out? No, I wasn't thrown out. They wouldn't do anything as uncivilised as that. But it was made plain to me that I had to choose between staying at the residence and visiting a certain man in his bungalow. So here I am."

A rush of words. Then she threw out her arms and ran to him. He stood his ground carefully as she pressed against him, put her head on his shoulder.

"I warned you about him," Gopala said.

"It was nothing like that."

He led her to a chair and sat down opposite her. He wanted the details of her conversation with Pat. He asked her to remember the actual words.

"Well, he said you could keep your job. Although you couldn't expect promotion. And he said, if you and I happened to meet on the compound, we could say hello to each other."

She thought her sarcasm was cutting, but it seemed to pass over him.

"It's not air-conditioned," he said, looking around, as if seeing where he lived for the first time. "The bathroom is not at all modern. And the kitchen needs …" His lower lip grew sumptuous with discontent as he contemplated the needs of the kitchen. She agreed with him. The bathroom could do with a good scrubbing and the kitchen was, well, spartan.

"At least you've got an indoor toilet," she said. "I won't have to run the gauntlet."

A flicker of distaste in his eyes did not register elsewhere, but he was not disposed to be jokey. They had a serious situation on their hands, which she did not seem to appreciate. If she had reported the gist of her talk with Mr Shard accurately, the assurances that his job would not be lost and that they could say hello to each other if they met on the compound only applied if she followed Mr Shard's advice, which was to stop visiting the bungalow. Not only had she declined the advice, but she had come to live at the bungalow.

"The residence will retaliate. Indeed, the compound as a whole."

She was scornful. "You make it sound like a state of war." She touched his arm. "This is just a small thing between the Shards and me. Anyway, they don't know I'm here."

"They'll find out. They find out everything."

They sat in silence without looking at each other. Then Annie stretched and stood up.

"Well, I'm hungry. And I can't think properly on an empty stomach." She moved towards the kitchen, which she did not know well. "Have you got something I can fix up quickly? Do you have a microwave?"

"Annie."

It was the first time he had used her name. The sound thrilled her and she waited, not daring to move. His voice had the even, insistent authority she remembered from the darkness by the pond. He walked across the room and placed his hands on her shoulders. He looked steadily into her eyes.

"I don't think it is wise for you to stay here."

She remained silent, waiting.

"Bifurcation," he said. "You have come to a fork in the road and you are taking the wrong direction."

He seemed deeply satisfied with his remarks and waited for her response, but her thoughts were practical. "Well, I'm here." She indicated her luggage, which remained where the servant had placed it.

"I'll take you to a hotel. You can have a good night's rest."

He smiled as he spoke. The thought of a good night's sleep seemed to have lifted his spirits. She pouted. "I'd rather stay here."

Actually, a thought had been niggling her. The bungalow did not seem right with her luggage in it. Her cases, one large, one small, and the shoulder bag she had bought at the bazaar, stood on the floor, out of place, looking as if they belonged somewhere else. The two cases were new, neatly matched in a fleur-de-lis pattern, and their elegant presence made the bungalow look shabby. It receded, became indistinct. It no longer came to meet her with invitations of intimacy and pleasure. The big teak bed looked gaunt. The two chairs and the circular table where they pretended to drink their tea looked uncomfortable, even unsafe. The wainscoting was dry and cracked, the floorboards scratched and stained. The ceiling sagged in one corner of the room.

"It's not wise," Gopala said, wagging his head. He left untold the wisdom he had in mind, but gave her some hope. "After you've had a good night's sleep, we can talk." His eyes brightened. "Evaluate options."

She remained silent. She had come to the bungalow because it had seemed the natural thing to do. They were in trouble together. Why not "evaluate possibilities" now? And she was hungry. Gopala was, however, already on the telephone, in the brisk Hindi he adopted to make arrangements. "Oh well," she said.

His relief was palpable, as if he had been wondering if she might shout and scream. Women often behaved badly when their emotions were upset.

"There's a small hotel in old Delhi that I've heard is good. Near Maiden's Hotel."

She laughed. "For maidens?"

But he was not to be distracted. He seated her at the little table and held her hands across it, assuring her that he would visit her at the hotel the following afternoon and that if she needed him in the meantime she only had to pick up the telephone, which he had no doubt would be provided in her room. It was a comfortable, efficient hotel, with a reputation for service. He gave her a number at the compound that would find him and warned her to telephone from the library or the hotel rather than to use her mobile, and then, when her irritation flared, conceded: if it was really urgent, she could. Having made that concession, he sat back and observed her with pleasure, as if they had together achieved something.

Before she had a chance to respond, she heard the familiar clank of a taxi engine and a blue turban appeared in the doorway. Gopala had been telephoning a taxi, not a hotel. And he was so anxious for her to leave that he picked up her luggage himself and carried it to the car. He bustled her swiftly into the back seat, nodded to the driver and stood at attention as the car departed with a squirt of pebbles.

A cold anger overcame her in the narrow, crowded streets of the old city. He had fobbed her off. He had not booked a room at the hotel. What was she supposed to do if the hotel was full? Or unsuitable, run-down like the bungalow, or worse? Wander around hunting for another hotel? Telephone him? She decided that if a room were not available, or the place was unsuitable, she would go to the swankiest place in old Delhi and let him find out for himself where she was. If a room were available, she wouldn't bother to inform him, either. She would not extend the courtesy of telling him she was safe and comfortable, if that highly improbable circumstance actually occurred.

But the small hotel was charming, friendly and clean and it did have a room that might have been prepared personally for her. She liked the pink and grey colour scheme, the painted calico curtains, the fluffy bed quilt, a high window opening onto a garden, the ceiling fan that turned quietly over her head. She had her own bathroom, containing a piece of purple English lavender soap.

It was called The Trilby. Under the nameboard hanging from chains at the front was inscribed "A Small Hotel". She changed into pyjamas and sat by the window. She could see the outline of the garden. In the middle was a big tree with sinuous, fleshy branches. They looped and drooped like elephant trunks, and she wanted to touch them. She felt embarrassed about going down to the courtyard alone at night, but the impulse was so strong that she could not resist it. She put on a gown and slippers and tiptoed down the narrow staircase. A man behind the reception desk noticed her and smiled in an accommodating manner. She approached the door opening into the garden and he slipped away from his desk and opened it for her.

Annie walked into the courtyard. She could feel rough ground and pebbles under her thin soles. She stumbled in the dark against some ceramic pots arranged in a circle around the base of the tree. Then she touched the tree itself. Its bark was soft and yielding, like skin. She ran her fingers along a low, smooth bough. Then she put her arms around the trunk, which was so broad where she stood that her hands only reached halfway around it. Nevertheless, she hugged it.

As she turned her head to improve her grip, she noticed the man standing in the doorway, watching her. She smiled at him and went on hugging the tree.

7

SHE WAS SITTING AT THE window in a rocking chair when he came.

She had noticed the chair on the first morning, poked away in a corner, when she came down for breakfast. Mrs Mehta explained in her lilting voice that it had been there when she first came to the hotel six, going on for seven, years before. It was a good piece of furniture and she had not wanted to throw it away, but she did not know what to do with it, so it remained where it was.

"Gathering dust and collecting cobwebs."

"If I clean it up, can someone take it to my room?"

"Good heavens, you don't need to clean it. We will certainly clean it. And, of course, if you wish to have it in your room, it will be carried upstairs accordingly. It will be no trouble at all."

Mrs Mehta was small and a bundle of energy, the sort of woman who might run a bed-and-breakfast establishment in Gippsland or the Blue Mountains, or perhaps in Scotland. She had never left India, but she had learned English "properly" at school and when the children were off her hands she had taken this job, at first part-time, now so full-time that she could barely find time for anything else. The hotel was owned by a business friend of her husband's. All this was conveyed woman-to-woman as she wiped the chair carefully with a wet cloth and as Annie ate her breakfast, which was not unlike what she had been given at the residence, even the silver toast holder.

So the chair, wiped clean and provided with a purple, embroidered cushion, was carried up the narrow stairs by one of Mrs Mehta's army of male assistants. Annie placed it at an angle to the window, so that when she sat in it she half-faced the door but could also see into the garden.

He stopped to catch the light on her face. He stood still as if he were storing the sight of her in his memory. Then he crossed the room and lowered his head and shoulders into her open arms. This was another of those times she would never forget. He knelt and she cuddled him. Something different, a tenderness, a need for forgiveness, had come over him. His hard passion was still there, but it was now pliant, weighty as water. His fingers were soft, his arms limp. She stroked his hair, murmured endearments. "Everything's alright." Scooping him closer. "There, there."

He was so quiet that after a while she thought he might have gone to sleep, but when she tried to disentangle him he shook his head and clung to her. So they stayed like this until the room became dark. Then suddenly he stood up, brushed and straightened his clothes, turned on the light and addressed her as if he had just entered the room.

"So you like it here. It was a good choice."

He was beaming with confidence and goodwill. He had shown her that his judgment was reliable. Not only was he knowledgeable about Indian culture and history, its seductive passions and turbulent depths, but also he was skilled in the sensitive area of a woman's comfort. If he had been carrying a walking stick, he would have twirled it.

"Where have you been?" It had been two days and three nights. Never mind. She scrambled from the rocking chair.

"Did you notice the garden? Come and see the bathroom."

They examined together the deep bath. He tested the hot water tap. She sniffed the lavender, fondled the curtain.

"Fancy having a chintz curtain in your bathroom," she said. "In India."

"It is from a Hindi word," he said. "Chint. The British adopted it. Like dekko."

Annie was impressed. Chintz was for her the essence of Englishness. She thought dekko was Australian. "She's nice, Mrs Mehta."

"Of course."

The Last Kiss

They went to a nearby restaurant. It was the first time they had been openly together in public. The restaurant was crowded, noisy and dark and they shared a large table, so there was no opportunity for intimacies other than eating. They had northeast frontier food, yoghurt, cucumber, Tandoori chicken, mutton and onion kebab, drank nimbu pani, lassi.

Then she led him back to her bedroom, up the narrow staircase. Mrs Mehta had gone home and the reception desk was occupied by one of her generals, who nodded cordially.

She had discovered at the library some love poems of Pablo Neruda. She read them to him, lying side by side on the fluffy quilt.

"Oh the bitten mouth, oh the kissed limbs,
oh the hungering teeth, oh the entwined bodies.
Oh the mad coupling of hope and force
In which we merged and despaired.
And the tenderness, light as water and as flour.
And the word scarcely begun on the lips.
This was my destiny and in it was the voyage of my longing,
And in it my longing fell, in you everything sank!"

She liked its directness. She wanted to extricate their passion from old Vidya's fairytale, but she could tell, from his fixed stare, that he disapproved.
"It is not lyrical."
"Well, it's a translation," she said, unsure what language Chileans used.
"So is Vidyapati, yet even so he is lyrical."
She coaxed him.

"Body of a woman, white hills, white thighs,
you look like a world, lying in surrender ...
I was alone like a tunnel. The birds fled from me,
And night swamped me with its crushing invasion.
To survive myself I forged you like a weapon,
Like an arrow in my bow, a stone in my sling."

Gopala was not impressed. "I have an early morning shift," he said, easing himself off the bed.

She did not want to spoil the memory of that moment in the rocking chair so she omitted two earthy lines that she thought might offend or unduly encourage him.

"My rough peasant's body digs in you
and makes the son leap from the depth of the earth."

He let himself out with raised hands at the door. It was the first time she had seen him off the premises. He was a daylight fixture in the compound; she came and went. At the bungalow, she was the one who had to leave. She was in his territory from the moment she arrived. The big teak bed was his. The bathroom of slimy cement was his, as was the bare kitchen and the creaking fan. He ravished her, and then, when he was satisfied lolled contentedly in his own place.

The small hotel was her territory. Not just the physical fact that she lived there and he was a visitor, but also that the style of the hotel, even its fussiness, pleased her. She felt at home; it was strange, because she had been escaping from fussiness all her life, but she did.

She wondered how their relationship might develop if she remained at Mrs Mehta's hotel. She had given herself to him in such an unguarded way that, in one sense, he knew her better than any other person in the world, although he knew nothing really about her. She hardly knew him at all. She could not imagine a sensible, professional conversation with him that would help her research. Well, at least he wasn't one of the galahs. She couldn't imagine him twisting a slender glass in his fingers. He wasn't a talking head, like the cockatoos.

Professor J.P. Ganguly paid a visit. He was a friend of Mrs Mehta's, or a friend of a friend. He often "dropped in" or "passed by".

"I'm not sure whether he is a professor of anything in particular," Mrs Mehta explained, "but he is very intelligent. People go to him for advice on all sorts of things. He's not a guru or a swami or anything like that. He's not at all religious. He's a scientific man. He's not floating around." She waved in the air, circling all those who were. "You'll like him. He's lively."

The professor had agreed to come to the hotel to meet Annie at afternoon tea. Mrs Mehta did not live at the hotel, but behind the reception desk was a small, sparely furnished room, including a couch on which she took her afternoon nap. It was in this room that she and Annie waited. French doors opened on the garden.

"It's not too cold yet. It's like an English spring!" Mrs Mehta's voice lifted when she referred to anything English. She was about to expand on English weather when the professor suddenly entered through the French doors.

"Good heavens!" said Mrs Mehta, her crisp voice excited by the unexpected. "I thought you would ring the reception bell."

"I did not notice it."

Why should one notice a small bell on a counter? And why, if reception is unattended, should one not go looking for one's hostess? She couldn't be far away. All of this was left unsaid by Professor J.P. Ganguly, although his manner implied it, and perhaps more. He stood there without further explanation, beaming back and forth at the two women. He was a neat, shining person, wearing sharply ironed trousers, toeless snakeskin shoes, a short-sleeved shirt and a bow tie. A computer bag was slung over one shoulder. He brought into the room an aura of cleanliness and efficiency, even goodness. He sat down after he and Annie were introduced to each other and waited to be asked questions.

"Annie is engaged on an interesting project which could have national, even international, significance," said Mrs Mehta.

It was not a question, although it invited a response. Annie, however, intervened quickly. "I don't know how this started, everyone keeps saying it … a project which could have national, even international, significance … but the fact is …" She realised that Mrs Mehta might be offended by the exact repetition of the phrase she had used.

"Of course, it's nice that people are interested and it might well turn out to be something of value, but I'm afraid it is as yet just a gleam in my eye, so to speak."

But the professor was disposed to disagree. "Madame, or should I say, mademoiselle, you are the epicentre of a verbal storm or, if I may slip into the vernacular, the talk of the town! Delhi is engulfed in a discourse that has but one topic, your estimable project, and but one subject, this venturesome antipodean archaeologist who arrives at the library each day not in limousine, not even in taxi, nor indeed in landau, barouche, brougham, hansom, cabriolet or char-à-banc, but in auto-rickshaw, even bicycle, like an ordinary Indian citizen."

Reeling, Annie managed to mumble, "They must have very little to talk about."

He listened respectfully to her deflating Australian voice but his deference was a springboard to higher flights of fancy. "On the contrary, and with respect, dear lady, Delhi is replete with interesting topics of bilateral or indeed multilateral verbal intercourse. Yet, everywhere I go, one topic simmers ... shimmers ... above all the others in this crockpot, indeed pressure cooker, of topical fervour. You will recall in Edward Morgan Forster's celebrated novel A Passage to India how the multitude murmurs incessantly the name of the English woman Mrs Moore, turning her into a Hindu goddess ... Esmiss Esmoor." He swayed his hips and crooned at her like a nightclub entertainer. "Esmiss Esmoor ... Esmiss Esmoor ... Rising and falling, rising and falling above all other sounds. Esmiss Esmoor!" He drew a long breath. "So it is now in Delhi, rising and falling above everything else, above the cocktail chatter, the parliamentary speeches, the radio, television, all other sounds ... Esmiss ..."

He stopped abruptly, as if his battery had died. "What is your good name?"

Appalled, yet captivated, Annie burst into scornful laughter. He took it in good spirit.

"I was carried away by the brilliance of my subject."

The professor smiled sweetly at each of the two women in turn, waiting for something else to claim his attention.

"Tell Annie about your own project," Mrs Mehta said loudly as she poured. "It's been in the newspapers and on the television," she whispered to Annie.

It was the professor's turn to be modest. "Oh, that was just the juicy bit."

Annie decided to play the role that Mrs Mehta had given her, to assist the professor to reveal himself in all his glory. "Juicy?"

"In India we are very decorous, very serious. The lighter part, shall I say. Less complex. More superficial. That sort of thing." He surveyed his little audience as if he had responded more than adequately to their needs. "The sort of thing the media likes."

"Such as?"

"Personalities. That sort of thing. Not the real issues."

"Which are?"

Annie was determined to extract something from him. He was just sitting there, smiling, taking her in and giving out nothing. Suddenly he raised his right forefinger.

"I have been thinking about the pool of Bethesda, according to the account in your Bible. There must have been something in the water that helped people with their ailments. I do not believe in miracles, of course. But the people believed it was a miracle. They believed that an angel appeared and troubled the waters and if they bathed, that they would be cured. Let us assume they were sincere. It is not important whether they bathed in the water because they believed in angels or because a doctor had told them to do so. The important question is: what was in the water?"

He moved his chair closer to Annie, looking at her intently. "In your country, you know what is in the water." Annie was tempted to make a crude remark, but he continued relentlessly. "In India we do not know what is in the water. We wash in it, bathe in it, drink it, worship it, but we do not know what is in it."

He smiled in his persistent manner, as if nothing more needed to be said, yet would nevertheless be stated in great detail by himself: "Too much religion, too many emotions. Too much feeling, not enough thinking. People bathe in the Ganges at Varanasi. Millions upon millions. They have no idea what is in the water. No doctor would tell them to bathe in those waters for their health. The waters are filthy but they are holy – and that is that. You might say, 'Oh well, this is a minor eccentricity, nothing to get upset about.' But it is not just what is in the water. Our agriculture, for example, is highly inefficient. Its success depends almost entirely on the weather! It consumes all our water in the dry months and is uselessly flooded in the wet months. Our production of food is cultural, not industrial, old-fashioned, not modern. Man has become a slave to what is planted in the ground and he worships gods who control the unaccountable fortunes of climate. Why should we continue this way, as if we had never heard of chemistry? Synthetic tyres, for example, are much longer wearing than tyres made from natural rubber. Synthetic fibre is much stronger than natural fibre.

Synthetic perfumes, synthetic dyes – these are all superior to the natural product. Quinine, morphine – the manufactured product is better. And so on. But in India we still behave as if traditional forms of agriculture are hallowed. So where is the modern India which was supposed to arrive when the colonial yoke was removed? It has not appeared. The yoke is still there."

This was a speech, but he scarcely needed the breathing space he had taken to extract a slim and shiny computer from his bag. He placed it on his knees and opened it. "We are still in the dark ages. There are 1.28 billion cattle in the world. That means there are 5.12 billion hooves tramping on the grass and probably 3.84 billion emissions of methane daily, contributing substantially to global warming. Yet in India the cow is a sacred animal!"

He continued, glancing up and down from the computer screen to the faces of the two women with barely a change of tone or pace. "Gold and magnesium from the oceans, saltpetre from the air, lubricants from sand. One hour's sunshine is worth a thousand combustion engines. One hour's sunshine, properly harnessed, is worth a thousand suns – remembering that it was the radiance of a thousand suns bursting into the sky, as described in the Bhagavad Gita as like the splendour of the Mighty One, that flashed through Robert Oppenheimer's mind when the first atomic bomb was exploded. Resources as free as the air! The modern world!"

Annie observed him with curled lip, unable to decide whether to laugh or turn off. His mind grabbed anything that floated past and made it his own, secreting clouds of broken thoughts. Well, at least he didn't repeat himself. "Your country invented the eight-hour day," said Professor J.P. Ganguly. "Now it must invent solar power after dark."

"You should go into politics."

"We are returning to the Middle Ages. The future is famine, poverty, social violence and religious wars. People talk about the danger of anarchy. In India it is already here. At long last, India is in the vanguard of history!"

He beamed possessively at Annie while swiftly typing and keeping an eye on the little screen. "On the other hand, your country is prosperous, scientific, secular and peaceful. The future there is creative leisure. In my country, we will catch up eventually with your eight-hour day, after industrial turbulence, political turmoil, social unrest – the lot, as you say.

But in your country, you will move steadily and peacefully to become a leisure society."

"You make it sound like heaven on earth," Annie interrupted. "I can assure you it's not. You can be as unhappy there as anywhere else on earth."

A keen observer would have noticed the fullness of Annie's lower lip, but Professor J.P. Ganguly was fixed on a higher objective. "Happiness! I do not speak of happiness. I speak of efficiency and effectiveness, what makes a nation successful in the modern world. Happiness is for children." He smiled. "And tender young ladies."

"That's the first time I've heard Australia called efficient," said Annie. "And you should meet our farmers. Our weather is just as inefficient as yours."

"Of course." Professor Ganguly beamed above his bow tie. "That's the whole point of the project," he said disarmingly. "To get at the issues."

"I'd be delighted to know what the issues are," said Annie icily, sitting upright with her hands on her lap and her feet close together. She had never liked bow ties. They were a sign of vanity.

"Of course," said Professor J.P. Ganguly. "We all would." His eyes sparkled with possibilities. He beamed relentlessly. His manner was deeply appreciative. Also, tucked away somewhere, he harboured thoughts he was not prepared to disclose. At least, not at this first meeting. He slapped shut his computer and prepared to leave.

"What kind of tree is that?" asked Annie, determined to make some use of him. She pointed to her tree in the garden.

The professor said he was an admirer of the aguru tree, a large evergreen with a fragrant scent, but only at its heart. "Externally it is nothing, but when you cut through ... it is like jasmine, delicious. As fragrant as the sandal. Santalum album."

He also liked the pipal (Ficus religiosa), because of its glossy, dark green leaves which shivered in the wind, and its shape, like a poplar. And the kimsuka (Butea frondosa), with its crimson flowers, herald of spring. However, if it was hard wood you wanted, the sisam (Dalbergia sissoo) was the best.

None of these, however, was the tree in the garden. He glanced at it quickly as he stood, bowed to Annie and departed buoyantly with Mrs

Mehta. "The human brain is like the roots of a tree," he called out on his way to the door. "The Romans had a forest god – Silvanus. Hence the word 'sylvan.'"

Annie was silent when Mrs Mehta returned, singing the praise of her remarkable friend. "I don't know how he keeps all that information in his head. He's like a computer. You press one button and out comes ... all this. You press another button and ..." She held up her hands. Anything might happen if you pressed another of Professor Ganguly's buttons. "And he's so kind-hearted," she said, clearing away the afternoon tea. "He will do anything for you once he's decided that you're ... well, that he likes you." She stopped, lost in thought, obviously one of his chosen people. "He's got a soft heart, a really soft heart. And warm hands, did you notice? It's not often that you find a man who is clever and kind. Not in India, anyway. Perhaps in your country. You're more like the English. But here, clever people are full of themselves."

8

She opened her diary and there it was. She had almost forgotten the conference. Today! Her heart jumped a couple of beats, guilt and then relief that she had noticed in time. She ordered a taxi at the front desk, bundled papers into a shoulder bag, changed into working clothes and was just in time at the National Museum building to catch a thoughtful opening address from the President of India on the role of the intelligentsia in developing societies.

The bustle of professional life brought a surge of confidence and contentment. Thinking outside the circle might be good for the mind but it was bad for the nervous system. Now she was again with people who knew the rules, even when they ignored them, and appreciated each other, even when they sought to undermine the work on which others had built their reputation. She crossed her ankles and settled back to enjoy the theatre of discovery and self-regard. She found herself, however, in an undertow of Indian self-absorption. In paper after paper, delivered with vehemence and style, a single theme surfaced, sometimes early and explicit, sometimes late and breathless. Up and down the scale, over and over again, it played throughout the conference like a signature tune. Indian and Greek civilisations were not, as she had imagined, a contrast; they were the same. For political purposes, India was Asian but in a deeper sense it was European, linked through the Aryans with Persia and the Mediterranean civilisations.

The Mahabharata was inspired by Homer's poems, and the influences worked the other way. Pythagoras, for example. His theory of transmigration of souls was obviously derived from India, and the idea of reincarnation, although some Western scholars were determined to trace it to Egyptian influence. His prohibition on eating beans was pure Indian. Plato was another case in point. His distrust of the senses and his belief in the reality of the form, or the idea, was quintessential Indian thinking, not Greek at all. The Greeks adored the body and physical beauty. It was obvious (to these scholars and as the day wore on she began to think, to her) that Plato was part of the development of thought in India, not in Greece. Indeed, India, not Greece, was the home of Western philosophy and therefore of the modern world.

The tone of the scholars was lofty, eloquent and aggrieved. The Indian philosophers who compiled the Upanishads were unknown, although they lived long before Plato or Confucius, who had become household names. So-called "New Age" thinkers in California trivialised Indian thinkers – often without attribution. How unfair it was! Like a baton in a relay race, they passed on from one speaker to the next the idea that India had been treated badly. The Western world had idealised the contribution to civilisation of the Mediterranean, especially the Greeks but also the Romans, and even the Muslims and the Jews, while that of India was overlooked. It was not only unfair; prejudice could not be discounted. The old enemy, neo-colonialism, was at work. Everyone knew about the threat of economic colonialism – and Indians were doing something about that. (Applause!) This was cultural, intellectual and moral colonialism. Something should be done about it. (Applause squared!)

The speakers were united in praise of the Aryans, whose origins, however, were obscure. Some thought they invaded India around 1500–2000 BC, at about the same time as Egypt and Mesopotamia fell into decline. Some maintained they came earlier from central Europe and southern Russia, and had spread both west, where the Celts, the Germans and the Greeks became their descendants, and east, settling in India and Iran. Either way, India was a winner. On the one hand, India existed before the Aryans. It was its own self. On the other hand, the Aryans connected Indians with the rulers of the modern world, the Europeans. You could see it in the aquiline

Indian face, compared with the flat faces and broad noses of Orientals (or Mongolians, as most of the speakers preferred to call them).

None seemed aware of the thin surface on which they were skating sublimely. The connection of Aryan genetics with the paranoia of Hitler and Nazi Germany was no more than a blip in the sweep of history they were juggling, if indeed they were aware of it at all. Annie bit her tongue and wriggled in her seat. A more practical problem for her was emerging.

She had begun her project with the general knowledge that the Harappan civilisation in the Indus Valley was contemporary with other early civilisations such as Egypt and Mesopotamia but, unlike them, it had not been dug over and sifted through by every budding archaeologist this century. So she had intended to find a site that, with her limited resources and time, she could work on her next visit. Perhaps in Harappa itself, on the Ravi River or one of the settlements at Lothal or Mohenjo-daro. Perhaps she could persuade the Archaeological Survey of India to take her on. The Indus Valley civilisation extended almost as far as Bombay (now Mumbai) and Delhi, including parts of Uttar Pradesh, Rajasthan and Gujarat. Political tension between India and Pakistan over terrorism in Afghanistan and Kashmir was a problem for any cross-border expeditions, so she wondered whether she might find a site that was easily accessible from Delhi. One possibility was Dholavira in Gujarat, securely inside India's borders.

The staff at the library had plied her with books about the range of Indian civilisation. She learned that Indus Valley relics (especially seals) had been found in the Tigris and Euphrates areas, as had semi-precious stones from Gujarat, metal from Rajasthan and food remnants from Baluchistan. Also, excavations in the Indus Valley had uncovered pottery, an adze and horned figures from Mesopotamia. She learned that Harappan writing resembled Egyptian script, and in both Egypt and India the worship of certain animals was common. Egypt had a social system similar to India's caste divisions. In both Mesopotamia and India men wore long beards but shaved their upper lips. They shared the swastika and the cross as religious symbols.

However, as the conference ploughed on, it became evident that initiative on the Harappan civilisation had moved from the archaeologists to the cryptographers. The relevant relics had been unearthed. Now it was a matter of deciphering the hieroglyphics on them, a question of language.

Everyone was excited by the possibility that this was a new language and even more excited by the possibility that this language might turn out to be the original script of the Aryans. If this were so, the Aryans might not have come to India, but begun there! She could see from the faces of the scholars that this was now the Big Question. Its implications were enormous, its impact momentous. It was not only of national, possibly international, significance. It was cosmic!

It was also bread and butter. By the end of the day, she was forced to draw the obvious conclusion. Honest diggers like herself were no longer in demand. Especially if they were foreigners.

At lunch, she shared a table with an Indian man with the red dot of Hindu religiosity on his forehead. "Please," he said, extending a hand towards a vacant chair as she looked around the crowded restaurant for a place to sit. He rose slightly from his own seat to support his invitation. Then he returned to his newspaper and his tea, like an English gentleman. Annie had been preparing to fend him off. She had already formed in her head courteous, uninformative replies to the questions she expected to be asked. But nothing happened. He slowly turned the pages of his newspaper with his left hand, as he sipped decorously from a cup held in his right.

She sat munching and sipping with lowered eyes, wishing she had something light to read. "What's the latest terrible news?"

He looked up with a quick smile, turning the pages of his paper, The Hindu, slowly back to the front page. "Oh, well, the usual." His smile twisted as he read. "Army alert. Terrorism. Cabinet meeting. That sort of thing. I'm from the south. Bangalore. It seems to be always like this when we visit Delhi." He straightened up and surveyed the room. "Delhi has a built-in threat detector, always on alert." He relaxed with a hint of apology, acknowledging her presence. "And you?" She told him, leaving out Gopala. "And what is your impression of our scholarship, also known as the great mind of India, to distinguish it from the great soul of India?" He put his head on one side, offering her an opening, but she chose caution.

"The Aryan heritage got a good run."

He chuckled. "It's a geo-political condition, a north India affliction, the holy grail of fair skin. Just look at the advertisements in the newspapers. And now on the Net. You would think that having a dark skin is a disease."

He told her that he was a drop-in at the conference, out of curiosity. He ran a master's degree course in Bangalore on information technology and was chairman of a start-up company in security services. He had recently decided to make engineering a prerequisite for his course and was in Delhi to lobby the central government for money.

"We are clever at maths and sciences. But we're not clever at applying knowledge. It stays in our heads, going in circles. As a Hindu, I understand our liking for abstraction. So I thought hands-on training, like engineering, would keep our feet on the ground. We want our students to be successful entrepreneurs, not just brilliant researchers. This is the lesson we have learned from Silicon Valley, where so many of our good people have gone. And it's working. More of our companies are doing well. But we do not have the private wealth of Americans. Most of their new companies fail, but they pick themselves up, take stock and start up again. We do not have that kind of money." He laughed. "I do not have that kind of money. So I come begging to Delhi."

"It's a help as a scientist being religious?" She implied by her tone of voice, if not the question itself, that she thought it might not be.

He pointed to the red dot on his forehead. "The tilak helps you to concentrate." He might have been inclined to leave it at that, a mechanical aid, but in deference to the entreaty in her voice was prepared to go further. "For a scientist, it helps if you're confident there's a connection between cause and effect. Your job is to find the connection. It doesn't really matter what propels you." His other arm encircled the universe. "The world is such a confusing place, it helps if you believe there's an explanation for it."

He glanced at his watch, gathered up his newspaper and excused himself, with the hope that they might meet again.

There was something so resolutely normal about him that Annie sat dreaming for a while after his departure. It was the first time in India that she had not felt baffled or annoyed by an encounter with an Indian male (leaving aside Gopala, in a category of his own). She wondered what her experience of India would have been if she had not been cocooned at the residence, if she had not turned her back and walked out that night at the pond, if there had been no Gopala, just people like Mrs Mehta and this man from Bangalore, with their safety net of common sense and good humour.

When the conference ended, they met by chance in the foyer. He was about to take a walk in Lodi Gardens. Would she like to accompany him? The gardens were excellent for conversation, he suggested, with an artless smile, while providing space for the mild exertion of degenerating bodies. Moreover, a borrowed Maruti was waiting to take them there. She accepted without a second thought.

It was a red car, glistening in the sun, and she slipped into the passenger's seat as if she had done it many times. He placed one hand lightly on the steering wheel and engaged gears with the other, as if he had been doing it all his life. Smoothly, the little car wound its way through the outskirts of the old city, and then buzzed along the wide roads of south Delhi. They chatted occasionally about the passing scene but most of the journey was in silence, which she enjoyed, pleased with the sensation that she was effortlessly going somewhere. He swung the car in a single movement to park alongside a police van, which had "With You For You Always" in red English lettering across its white panels. He raised his eyebrows. "The state and the market are uneasy companions."

Annie had been taken to the Lodi Gardens by Pat and Iris on her first day in India, and had liked them immediately. They were sensibly laid out, with picnic spots, jogging tracks and walking paths over arched bridges in old brick. It was a place for lovers, the only public space in India where she had seen men and women snuggling and cuddling, not just holding hands. But it was the 500-year-old tombs of the Lodi kings, who had come from Afghanistan to establish an empire ruled from Delhi, that she remembered. They were scattered through the gardens like giant sentinel boxes, guarding the past.

He was a brisk walker. "Just for ten minutes. Then we can slow down and look at the tombs." She kept pace with him, moving into single file, sometimes in front of him, sometimes behind, when they encountered other brisk walkers on the narrow path. Occasionally he would point wordlessly at something which no doubt he intended to explain later – a tree, a small mosque glimpsed through a grove, a turreted wall, an expanse of water, a gathering of children in school uniform. They emerged from a thicket and across a sloping lawn was one of the tombs. He slowed down, turning to her. "This is the oldest."

"Whew!" Grateful, Annie bent over to catch her breath. "I'll have to stop smoking."

"Yes," he said. "You should." It was a statement of fact, a judgment without prejudice.

The gardens were relatively new, he explained, created as Lady Willingdon Park, after the viceroy's wife, an "unintended consequence" (he smiled) of an attempted renewal by the British of the imperial idea in the 1930s, when the English architect Sir Edwin Landseer Lutyens turned from restoring county manors and cathedrals at home to building a magnificent house in classical style for the viceroy in New Delhi. "It was a bit late" (the same smile) for the empire (he left her to juggle the dates), but the beginning of a revival for the Moghuls. Before then, the tombs had been left unattended, as ruins in the bush, for hundreds of years. Now they were renovated as ornaments of another imperial presence. After independence, the park was renamed Lodi Gardens, after an Afghan chief and adventurer who moved in to take over from the Turk conqueror Tamerlane, famous for his bloody sacking of Delhi, and landscaped to accommodate not just the tombs but trees and plants from all over India, and even outside. "The secular internationalism of the new India, Nehru's India," he said, by way of conclusion.

Had she noticed the gums? And there was also wattle, bottlebrush, grevillea and casuarina (called whistling pine) from Australia, frangipani and mesquite from central America, conifer from eastern America, magnolia from southern America, palm from Cuba, kapok from the Amazon. Her guide regarded the point as having been made.

As for the tombs, he was an admirer, even if they were the resting place of conquerors who for all their military and political power had never been able to subdue the true spirit of India, the Hindu south. Indeed, not even northern India. Rajasthan, for example, was unaffected by Muslim rule. "All that delicate colour and sinuous movement," he said dismissively. "All those rajahs and maharajas."

They stood inside a domed chamber looking out through a verandah of arches.

"The Moghuls gave us the arch," he pointed out, "which they had learned to build from the Romans. We were struggling with lintels, narrow doors and halls crowded with supports. They gave us space and elegance. A revolution in engineering." He chuckled. "We are fortunate in having been conquered by practical people. The British gave us the railways."

She did not know whether he was savouring the unlikely connection between the Muslim invaders from the north and his course on information technology run by a religious Hindu in the unsullied south, the stupidity of religious bigotry, the simplicity of technological progress or the discomfiture of fundraising. But she chuckled with him, instinctively taking his arm as they strolled back to the little red Maruti.

It was a human response, partly to avoid potholes and tree roots, but it was also, she realised, a gesture of companionship. She did not normally take the arms of men, or for that matter, women, but here in India, and especially in a garden that was also a grave and a memorial, it was good to be reassured that the human mind was resilient, that being alive was not just living in the present, but managing it by understanding the past.

In the Maruti on the way back to the hotel, she asked him again about the obsession of Indian scholars with Aryan heritage.

A thought surfaced, perhaps not for the first time. "We need to be conquered by a race of darkies!" But, where were they? "The Chinese are light-skinned, the Russians sallow, the Pakistanis much like us. The Africans don't have the technology to be imperialists." Hands in the air, off the steering wheel, not long enough to cause alarm, and their effortless journey continued. He dropped her at The Trilby, apologising for monopolising the conversation. "Next time, you can tell me what it's like to live in a land without history." He made it sound like a compliment. They exchanged business cards and she realised they had been together for a couple of hours without knowing each other's name. It did not seem to matter. She could not remember, when the red Maruti disappeared down the driveway, how he was dressed, although she had noticed that his skin was as dark as Gopala's.

9

ANNIE WOKE BECAUSE OF SIRENS and flashing lights. She lay awake listening, then the hubbub lapsed, the night took over and she went back to sleep. When she went downstairs for breakfast, everyone was talking about it. People a few buildings down the street had been arrested. A night curfew had been imposed. No one could be on the streets after 8 pm.

"What's it all about?" Annie asked.

"There's a threat," said Mrs Mehta. "To ..."

"National security," said one of her generals.

"Stability," said another, reading a newspaper. "There's no direct mention of security in the prime minister's statement."

"Well," said the first general, "it's certainly implied that external enemies could take advantage of internal political instability."

"Anyway," said Mrs Mehta. "There's an emergency."

That seemed beyond dispute. They were even discussing security measures for the front door. But Mrs Mehta was reassuring.

"There's no need for you to worry, dear. It's just one of those Indian things." She waved a hand. "It will go away. Just go to the library as if nothing has happened." She became thoughtful. "Of course, no social life. After 8 pm, I mean."

At the library, the girl with the shiny hair was bubbling with information. "All bags must be searched. We also have authority to search persons reasonably suspected of being dangerous." She was excited at the prospect of searching dangerous people. She whispered to Annie. "How do you know if they're reasonably suspected of being dangerous?"

Annie could not concentrate. It was strange to be sitting quietly reading, when the world outside was turning upside down. She remembered what it was like in school, trying to take lessons seriously when all you wanted to do was to get outside and race about. Returning early to the hotel, she thought of telephoning Pat. He would explain it all sensibly, but she did not feel she was in a position to seek a favour and she did not want to disclose her whereabouts. She needed Gopala and was relieved when he arrived early.

"Delhi is a boiling cauldron," he said.

"Boiling cauldron?" She wanted real information, not metaphors, but he was in authority mode and brushed her quibble aside. "It's not the heat you have to watch. We know in India how to deal with heat. It's the bubbles, the puffs of air as they rise to the surface, that cause trouble. That is where the instability starts. The little puffs."

"So what can be done about the little puffs?"

Her irony floated over his head. "You must stir, keep stirring. Stirring exposes the bubbles to the air and prevents them from forming into little puffs. The bubbles are still there, but stirring reduces their size and their number, so you get turbulence, which is annoying but stable, provided you keep stirring. You keep stirring until the heat drops and the surface returns to normal, which is a kind of simmer. Simmering can be managed."

"What stage are we at now?"

"The stirring has just started."

"Who is doing it?"

"The authorities, of course."

"Who turned up the heat?"

"Terrorists."

"What sort of terrorists?"

"Probably Muslims."

They sat on either side of the window, angled to each other, while the sun reclined in spreading pink behind them. Annie rocked herself gently, while Gopala marshalled all he knew about the emergency, as if he were a general addressing a staff meeting. Counterterrorism was like an earthquake: the tremors magnified as their distance from the centre increased. Here, at the centre, action was controlled. Out in the regions, in the villages, the world of his father, turbulence became turmoil. His father would be counting the arrests, noting the paybacks, watching the till. The border regions were always a worry, especially those shared with Pakistan, where the terrorists had sanctuary, but there was also concern about the heartland.

He became thoughtful, eyes downcast and head turned away, as if posing for a portrait. "So you are having an Indian experience," he said. "Like visiting the Taj Mahal. Or Khajuraho." His words were on stilts, rising one above the other. "Or Mahabalipuram."

"Where?" Her voice was flat and aggressive.

"I thought an archaeologist would have it on her list of Indian attractions." He was admonishing, defying the glint in her eye. "You know Bali of course." He made common knowledge of Bali seem improper. "Mahabalipuram is big Bali, the original. Here, within sound of the sea, is the Dravidian architecture and rock sculpture that inspired the builders of Angkor and Borobudur. From here, the great merchant princes of India despatched their fleets to your part of the world." His sarcasm was so eloquent it was almost tender. "I hope I have it right. It is your part of the world?"

He was aggrieved, and she reached out to him. A small hand fumbled, searched for one of his and held it. But his pride had propelled him to his feet.

"There is the wheel of life," he said, "and there are wheels within wheels."

"What's that supposed to mean?"

"The mystery of action," he said. "On the eve of battle, Arjuna asks, 'What is the difference between winning and losing?' And the answer he is given is, 'None.' True action in the world, leading to enlightenment, must be taken without attachment to the result, without desire or anxiety. Self-motivated action is spiritual death."

Annie sighed. "Who told him that?"

"Krishna."

"Not that Krishna again," said Annie. She had picked up a brush and comb and was tending her hair. "He's been got at by the other side."

Gopala moodily watched her. She ran a comb along each side of her head and up from the nape of her neck, then brushed the top, back and forth. Her energy absorbed him. He looked irritable, even envious, as if he wished he also had something to do, but could think of nothing except propping himself on the bed and watching her.

He protested. This was the Bhagavad Gita, one of the great sources of Indian wisdom, derived from thousands of years of people living together. Culture was the result of reflecting on human experience and in India a lot had happened to a lot of people. In fact, everything had happened. India's experience of warring states and families, the human cost of conflict and its political resolution – all these were as substantial in India as any in human history. Nothing had not happened in India! That was what the Mahabharata was all about. That was why the Indian statesman Kautilya was able to say what Europeans like Clausewitz and Bismarck and Metternich did not understand until centuries later.

"And that is why Indians put knowledge above work and harmony above action."

Gopala's words washed over Annie. "If you're going into battle, you've got to give yourself a chance. Or why bother?" Her knowledge of military strategy was rudimentary, but she knew fatalism when she saw it.

"Indians are quite capable of winning." He was prim and tart now, requiring him to stand and deliver. "We win cricket and hockey matches quite satisfactorily, even at times decisively. Our athletes are addicted to the acquisition of gold, silver and bronze medallions. Our soldiers are more than accustomed to winning wars. We have nuclear weapons, not because we were given the knowledge or the materials by someone else, hoping to make us their proxy, but from our own resources. Indians are very self-reliant. Our scientists and business leaders, in open competition with the rest of the world, are as good as any. Our legal system is adversarial and our politicians are as energetic in pursuit of their interests and as combative as any in the world. Our media is independent and critical, some think excessively so."

"Whew!" said Annie. Diminished, she stopped brushing her hair, but refused to be distracted. "That's what I was saying. In the real world, no one believes all that stuff about losing being good for you."

"We are humbled by victory." Gopala was now heading for the door, from where he turned to make another announcement. "Our soldiers do not wish to humiliate the enemy. They respect him. When they are victorious, our sports men and women do not thrust their faces at their opponents, pointing rudely at them, ordering them off the field, taking off their shirts and hugging themselves in jubilation, showing off for the television cameras. Our politicians are antagonistic, even fiercely so, but they do not belittle each other, mock each other. They are engaged in serious work, so while they oppose each other in deadly earnest, one does not question the integrity of the other."

Annie accepted the rebuff. Her father was like that; he couldn't stand sledging in cricket, playing to the gallery, celebrity culture, all that accusing and braying in parliament. It was American, not Australian, according to him. Americans were "up themselves" and Australians were getting to be not much better. She had been meaning to send her father a postcard ever since she arrived, but she could not think what to write on it that would please him. Now Gopala was providing a phrase or two.

He was not finished. "You make fun of our English, but we have turned the tables. We have global call centres, pretending to be American, Canadian, South African, Australian. Even British, the creators of the English language. We are excellent mimics. It is a thriving industry, good pay and working conditions. Look at the advertisements in the local papers."

Pumped with pride, he reminded her of army officers of the British Raj in black-and-white films, faced with a truculent demand for India's independence. Not quite the red-faced colonel's "Inja!" but certainly the clipped tone of the seasoned old hand. "Indiuh!"

"Yes suh!"

He looked at her long and hard and then spoke in a modest and conciliatory tone of voice.

"Would you not agree that, either way, it is an excellent outcome? If you go into battle knowing that the result is immaterial, fight gallantly and win, it is all the better. And, if you lose, it is still good."

"It might be alright for you, in your poetic head, but you're ignoring psychology." Annie was enjoying a verbal bout in which they were equals. "What about the troops down there on the ground. They need to know why they are fighting. It's not a game. They might be killed."

"Psychology." His face took on the benign gravity of a chess player who has been provided with a clearway to the king. "In India the fantasies in peoples' heads are kept in place not by considerations of victory or defeat, or moral assessments of right and wrong, but by duty."

"You mean caste?" She was severe and precise, determined to say what she meant and mean what she said.

He punched the air, repelling her insistence and celebrating at the same time. "It's a miracle!" He stopped and raised his hands in the air. "The logic is inescapable. If you want to change society, you have to abandon caste."

"So it's a rort."

"Rort?"

"A confidence trick."

He considered the possibility, pacing his thoughts as he moved about the room. "No, it is not rort." He turned, raising one forefinger. "Not rort, but Catch-22." Pleased by his facility with popular culture, he would now demonstrate its serious benefit.

"Our soldiers know their place. Caste keeps the military in line. Their job is to defend the country, not run it."

She could see his mind whirring and waited for the click.

"Indians are protected by the caste system from the populist appeal of a leader on a white horse who promises to obliterate the social resentments and rivalries that are a product of the caste system." He paused to relish the exquisitely balanced confinement of what he had said. "It is a miracle!"

"It's a con." A sturdy humanist defending the rights of ordinary men and women, she did not feel the need to elaborate.

He ignored her. "In Pakistan, the army is always taking over. In other countries also. In India, the army keeps its place, even when the politicians squabble and the people are yearning for action."

Annie was silent, not wishing to relinquish her position by straying into the outskirts of his.

"Everything is straightforward in your country, isn't it?" He avoided disdain, but his inquiry did not call for a response. "In India, nothing is straightforward. Nothing is what it seems. It is always something else. It is there – and it is not there."

She observed him calmly, as if he were describing a common occurrence.

"Sometimes in my poems I have to stop and ask myself, 'What is it?' " He opened his hands to show his helplessness.

"God knows," she said. "That's why I wanted to be an archaeologist. You dig it up. Then you know what it is."

He remained baffled. "But when you have found it, you still have to decide. What is it? A chip off a cup? Or a way of life? An answer to the mystery?"

"What mystery?"

"The mystery of the truth," he said, smiling at a fellow traveller on the journey of life.

"First reality, now the truth. You're playing for high stakes."

"People hardly ever tell the truth." It was a bald statement, yet scarcely bold, and he set about giving it a focus. "When you want to get at the truth, it's always something to do with someone else. But if it's something to do with you, well, that's different."

"You mean I don't tell the truth."

"Not just you, everyone. We pursue the truth when it is someone else's truth, but when it's ours, we prefer to cover it up, or leave it uncovered."

Annie was thoughtful. "Speak for yourself."

"We want to protect ourselves. We don't want people to know us, really and truly, because if they did, we would be possessed by someone else. Someone would be able to manipulate us, control us. So we don't tell the truth about ourselves. We mislead people instead. We give them false clues, to put them off the scent. To protect our identity. That's what we do. Isn't it?"

Yes, she thought, that's it. You never tell people what you really want, what you really feel. Let them work it out for themselves. Including now. It was time to stop this conversation. She stood. He accepted the cue and moved to the door.

"My father said you should help those less fortunate than yourself," he announced.

This was surprising. The father had been merciless before. "He's trying to get a good possy for himself next time around," she suggested. "Reincarnation."

Gopala was unmoved. "Is anything wrong with that?"

"Nothing. Nothing at all." She just managed to get the words in before the door slammed.

10

WHEN ANNIE WENT DOWNSTAIRS IN the morning, she learned that Mrs Mehta had been "detained". Two of her generals had been taken away with her. She was in her room at the back of the reception desk when two police entered without knocking. Within a few minutes they came out, followed by Mrs Mehta. She walked from her office to the waiting car without a word to her staff.

Gusts of information swirled around the foyer. Professor Ganguly had also been "apprehended", a surviving general thought, although he could not explain why he thought so. He had "heard", he said mysteriously, as if the information had come to him as a whisper on the wind. He had also "heard" that Mrs Mehta's husband had been "whisked off". He could not explain the difference between being "detained", "apprehended" and "whisked off", but he repeated the phrases diligently.

An envelope had been slipped under the door of her room. Inside was a single sheet of paper, on which was written:

"The fragrance of flowers
Enters the city,
Bees sing,
The moon and night enchant,
Yet all are enemies."

No signature. The ominous tone of the poem caught her mood; the pulse that used to start beating at the thought of Gopala was still. At the library, she turned pages mechanically and looked up anxiously whenever a door opened. She returned to the hotel early and stayed in her room, seated in the rocking chair, staring out the window, worrying about Mrs Mehta, wanting her to turn up suddenly saying it was just one of those irritating things that happen in India and should not be given a second thought, puzzling over Professor Ganguly, hoping that he would poke his head around the door, gleaming at her. But nothing happened. And Gopala did not come.

Another pawed and bedraggled envelope arrived. From its appearance, it might have been crinkled between heavy thumbs, its flap wetted and teased to see if it might open, held up to the light, rattled to see if it contained anything interesting.

She opened it in the rocking chair by the window and read:

"I am going today, dear friend,
And shall not fear the elders at home.
Words will not trouble me ...
I shall cover my body in white
And walk with leisured steps ...
From staring eyes I shall not flinch
Nor shall I hide.
So much did I conceal
From fear of others,
Even the currents of my love."

He was up to something. She was beginning to learn the signs. He had decided to act. Would it be direct and with purpose, as normal people acted, or would it be without desire or anxiety for the result, according to the Bhagavad Gita? Annie went to bed, lying flat on her back looking at the ceiling, with the blanket pulled up to her chin. What was he up to?

In a manner that was almost imperceptible, the staff turned to her in Mrs Mehta's absence. The surviving generals were reluctant to take responsibility for anything while the emergency lasted. Perhaps they were irresolute by temperament or Mrs Mehta's "detention", which they understood to be less rigorous than being arrested but more serious than "apprehension", made them nervous, but they encouraged Annie to believe they would like her to make decisions. They did not seek her assistance directly, but lesser members of the staff did and when Annie prudently raised matters for decision with the generals, they smilingly agreed.

The question of hot milk at breakfast. It was used both for porridge, which Mrs Mehta maintained in defiance of the common hotel trade in miniature packets of cereal, and for coffee, which was served, south-Indian style, in long-handled copper containers. For some reason, milk was in short supply and each day loomed as a crisis for the small hotel's much vaunted and valued breakfast service. They had tried condensed milk once, with low approval ratings. Annie proposed milk powder, with slightly less water than recommended, to give it body, and stirred briskly with an eggbeater to make it froth. With a pinch of salt and a dollop of butter, it was a success with the porridge-eaters and even, with doses of sugar, with the coffee-drinkers. From this, Annie graduated to more serious decisions. When should the fire in the sitting room be lit? The later the better, because wood also was scarce. On the other hand, guests did not want to sit in their rooms until dinner and the small hotel prided itself on being able to provide a congenial atmosphere in what were described in its modest publicity brochure as its "public rooms". Annie proposed a late time, to the generals' satisfaction.

She attended to guests at the front desk. She learned how to check them in, select a room, hand over the key. Sometimes she would answer the telephone. "The Trilby – A Small Hotel!" She smiled self-consciously the first time she said it, but it became as natural as her own name.

She entered Mrs Mehta's private room, behind the reception counter. It was just as she remembered it from her encounters with Professor Ganguly. Three chairs were placed around the table as they had been that first afternoon. She opened the French doors into the garden. The sweet smell of bark and leaves and moist soil came to her. She walked around the room, examining the pictures on the walls. They were formal – Mrs Mehta being greeted by a government minister on some official occasion, the generals all standing to attention, the small hotel festooned in banners, presumably at its opening; a section of the military parade down Rajpath on India's national day.

Annie realised how little she knew Mrs Mehta. They had quickly become friends because they had liked the look of each other and had proceeded with their relationship without bothering to discover any of the personal details friends normally know. Mrs Mehta had provided the bare bones of a curriculum vitae in a burst of confidences at the beginning, but since then she had said nothing about herself or her family. Annie had met only Professor Ganguly, whatever that meant.

11

HE CAME IN THE MIDDLE of the night. She woke with a start and trembled. He knocked again, a few raps more than before, gently insistent, appealing. She turned on the bed lamp, sat up straight and called out firmly, as if it might be a stranger.

"Who is there?"

She strained in the silence and his voice came, faint and precise.

"I am there."

He burst in impatiently, lightly brushing her aside, closing the door behind him with one hand, a bag in the other. "I was caught in the curfew."

Annie went back to bed, warm and secure. She left him standing in the middle of the room, watching her, his eyes intense and direct.

"You got my note?"

"I got another bit of Vidya."

"It is not wise to write directly."

But now he was here, with an overnight bag in his hand, standing in the middle of the room.

"What do you mean, caught in the curfew?" He was always so punctilious.

Gopala did not respond. He looked stolidly at the bag as if it contained the answer.

"Did you know Mrs Mehta is in gaol?"

He nodded in resignation. "There's an emergency."

"Yes, but Mrs Mehta!"

"Lots of people are detained in an emergency." His face assumed a sorrowful expression, mask of the Indian people's suffering. "It's part of our history. Nehru spent a lot of time in detention."

"Yes, but Mrs Mehta, for God's sake!"

"He did his best writing in gaol. He said it was good for concentration."

"That was the struggle for independence."

His eyes strained to catch her meaning, which she waved away.

"People like Mrs Mehta shouldn't go to gaol. What has she done?"

"Who knows?"

He shrugged his thick shoulders. Who could say what mysterious couplings of cause and effect had pointed the authorities in the direction of Mrs Mehta? "Who knows what she might have done? Or might not have done?"

"Might not have done?"

He was silent. He did not know what Mrs Mehta might not have done.

"You think sending people to gaol is good for law and order? Makes people feel safe? Whose side are you on?"

They could not go on with this conversation, she in bed, he standing in her bedroom with an overnight bag in his hand. She could not throw him out, the way he had thrown her out. There was a curfew and it was the middle of the night. He, too, would be "apprehended". So she invited him into her bed. It seemed the right thing to do. There was no sofa, the two chairs wouldn't make a bed and she couldn't put him on the floor. He had come prepared to stay. As soon as she issued the invitation, he retired to the bathroom, emerging in navy blue pyjamas and a smell of mint-flavoured toothpaste.

It was the first time they had literally slept together and they kept apart. Unlike the big teak bed, this one had inner springs and firm contours, suggesting space and inviting separation, not entanglement. They did not even kiss each other goodnight. He turned his back and was quickly asleep. She woke several times during the night, unaccustomed to his still, distant body near her.

He woke with the first slice of daylight, slipped from her bed, showered and changed into khaki trousers and a cream shirt with the collar embroidered in orange thread. "Good morning!" he announced from the bathroom door. He skirted the bed, opened the window and admired the big tree while she slowly became aware of him. The tree was topped with early morning gold and she first saw him with a halo of sunbeams around his head. "Good morning," she croaked from her pillow. She closed her eyes to hold the moment. This was the first time he had seen her in bed in the morning. She felt peaceful knowing he was in the room. All passion gone, a kind of courteous intimacy remained. At any moment now he would ask her what she would like for breakfast.

But he needed to shave, for which he had brought the necessary equipment. The smell of the cream on his face came to her in waves of childhood memory, yet the black-statue body with foam-whipped face was unmistakably Gopala. He had left the door ajar and she could see his eyes in the mirror. They were rimmed with pink above the white.

He turned his face slightly, acknowledging her presence. "Lord Krishna's domestic arrangements were unusual." He explained that Krishna had been born into a princely family, but a tyrant king (the demon Krishna had been born to destroy) had imprisoned his parents and they had given him to a cowherd family to bring up. His first loves were gopis, women cowherds who were actually married women with cowherd husbands.

"Gopala," Annie said, in a serious voice. It was the first time she had used his name.

He was silent, scraping white froth from shining black. He examined parts of his face that the razor had missed, finding it necessary to lather again under his nose; his upper lip was now so contorted it was impossible for him to speak. She waited, patient, even dutiful. He would have to answer eventually, which he did.

"Yes."

"Let's stop this Krishna and Radha nonsense. What's going on? You are up to something."

He wiped his face with her handtowel, gathered up his things, placed each carefully in his bag, glanced at his watch. Except for his overnight bag, he might have been an Indian husband hurrying to get to the office on time. But, instead, he came to her bedside and took one of her warm, pink hands in his. Then he stepped back and in a dramatic monologue, half speech, half reverie, opened his heart.

"I have a family to keep. We have three girls in our family and my father does not have a good salary. I won an essay competition in our local newspaper. It got me the job at the high commission. I had risen to a position where the salary was fair and the hours were flexible, so that I could work on my poetry. I had decided to be a celibate poet. I wanted to break with normal life completely. I accepted my family responsibilities, but nothing more. I wanted the time and the solitude to think about the mystery of life. If I had had more courage, I would have become a mystic and lived in the mountains. In my head I did. I was able somehow, working at the compound and writing in my bungalow, to live at different levels at the same time."

He was alert, as if he had made a decision and would not be distracted from its consequences. The distant look had gone. His eyes did not swivel, his body was not contorted, his smile did not hover. His language was clear and direct. She could actually understand what he was saying. She waited for him to recoil. She waited for the nip-and-tuck, the word of the father, the click. None of them came. He should have been quoting by now the Bhagavad Gita, or relapsing into a brooding silence, flung over a chair, erupting into incomprehensibly precise questioning. Instead, he stood upright before her and poured out his thoughts.

"Then you came to me that night at the pond, I could not believe it was happening, you came from nowhere, you were a gift from the gods. You changed my life. You overturned my world. Before you came I was living like a monk, cut off from the world."

She parried him. "You make it sound like punishment."

"It was like a bolt of lightning. Everything fused. Everything came together. You, me, Vidya's poetry, Radha and Krishna. Everything. The poetry became real, Radha and Krishna became real, we became real."

She lowered her head in defeat. He saw the back of her head, the parting as her hair fell away, her white neck, her freckled shoulders. An image that had been forming in her mind since their first encounter on the big teak bed burst through.

"You're no monk. You're one of those ..." Her writhing arms demonstrated. "... yogis."

He smiled obliquely, but continued. He had a message to deliver. "India is heading for trouble." There, he had said it. His secret was out. No more evasions, elisions, allusions, double meanings, explanations designed to hide the truth. He smiled, as if a weight had gone from his shoulders. She waited, as if a small stone had been thrown into a big pond. He moved into a higher gear, raising an interlocutory finger.

"Bollywood has taken over India. India is now Bollywood, like America. Hollywood has taken over America."

He paused, as if that might be enough, but Annie gave no indication that his message had reached her.

"For the world, Hollywood is America. Wealth and power, glitz and glamour, murder and mayhem. For the world, Bollywood is India. Wealth and power, glitz and glamour, murder and mayhem." He paused, allowing the single image of the two nations, worlds apart, to settle. "But not just the world!" He shrugged off the world with a movement of his shoulders. "India and its people. Bollywood is the new reality, the new Indian identity. Not the Gita, not the Upanishads, not the philosophy that winning in a brutal world is as onerous as losing, not the secular humanism of Nehru, not the passive resistance of Gandhi, not neutralism, non-alignment and the new international order. None of these."

His voice was still high, but he had become almost too burdened with sorrow to continue, to say what had to be said. He braced himself.

"Making money and making bombs. And playing the fun and sex game. The lowest common denominator of sensation. Long close-ups of kissing. That is the new India."

The thought was tearing him apart. And he had not finished.

"And here are these Muslims, simple fellows saying that the system is sinful because it lives off the labour of the poor, that democracy debauches the human spirit by putting desire and self-interest above the teachings of the prophets, that women baring their flesh in public are immoral and gambling and strong drink are symptoms of social decay, that modern life is artificial and to be authentic we must go back to the words of wisdom, which in their case is an updated version of the words of the Supreme Being of wrath and vengeance in your Old Testament."

"Not mine."

He paid no attention. He was nearing the end of his message, and the end of his tether. His body subsided. He looked around the room for somewhere to sit, propped himself against the bed.

"They are right. And it's not just Christian Westerners who are in the firing line, nor the Jews in Israel. It's Hindu infidels as well." He caught a fleeting thought. "You will have noticed that the servants at the High Commissioner's residence are Muslim. That's a legacy of the British. They used the Muslims skilfully as allies against the Hindu princes."

She hadn't noticed. How could you tell? They weren't religious. She had never seen them praying. They shaved. One of them was a rascal with young women.

He dragged himself to his feet, looked around for his bag, surveyed the room with a deep breath. Then he moved quickly to her bedside, brushed her cheek with a light kiss, and was gone.

For the first time since the pond, she wondered if she would see him again.

12

SHE DECIDED TO VISIT MRS Mehta in gaol. She took a taxi, giving the address in an outer suburb with a show of bravado, although when they reached the prison, with its high cream walls, turreted corners and armed guards, she trembled at the thought of entering. She gave her name at the security gate and entered the compound, which was shaded with gumtrees. The effect on her of the eucalypt smell was overwhelming; they looked strong and beautiful in a forsaken place. Her eyes were moist with ridiculous tears.

The woman who came to the busy, desolate space where prisoners and visitors met had changed, pared down to an anxious and timid person. The quick hand and eye connections that had given Mrs Mehta's movements a flirty quality had been stilled. Her eyes were dull, her hands hung by her sides or, when she sat down, rested in a listless clasp on her lap. Annie wondered if she was drugged.

She had bought some mangoes and a posy of marigolds, which Mrs Mehta accepted without comment.

"Do they feed you properly?"

"They don't starve you." She sat with eyes downcast, like a student in dunce's corner.

"But it's not exactly home cooking?"

Mrs Mehta burst into tears. Each sob was heavy, deep and long. She put her elbows on the metal table and cupped her face in her hands. Her shoulders heaved, her body trembled. The woman on guard over their conversation was unmoved, so Annie came to the other side of the table and put an arm around Mrs Mehta's back, while she stroked her hair with her other hand.

"Everything will be alright," she said. "Don't worry."

Mrs Mehta's sobs subsided. She sat up, wiped her eyes with her fingertips and managed a thin smile.

"You think it will be alright?"

"Of course." What else could one say?

"You have something in mind?" Mrs Mehta asked hopefully.

Annie had nothing in mind. She had come not because she had anything to say but because she felt Mrs Mehta had been treated badly and because she was fascinated by the appalling idea of her in gaol. In the back of her mind was the possibility that Mrs Mehta would explain why she had been detained, arrested, apprehended or whatever it was that had happened to her. But for Mrs Mehta, Annie's visit was a lifeline. She saw her visitor as someone with influence in the world outside, who had connections with those who were civilised and sensible.

"They wouldn't dare do this if I had a British passport."

Her voice was subdued, so that she sounded as if she were complaining, not defiant.

"Is there anything I can do?"

Mrs Mehta might have been disappointed that Annie was lacking in plans to get her out of gaol, but even in her present circumstances, she was still a generous woman with a practical mind.

"You shouldn't be putting yourself out. It's good of you to help at the hotel. I hear you've made yourself very useful."

Her wistful, thoughtful manner was an emotional hazard, Annie thought, so she responded cheerfully.

"If someone at the hotel asks me to do something, I do it if I can. That's all. It's the least I can do."

The last sentence created, however, a tremor in her voice and Mrs Mehta again burst into tears.

"There, there."

As she again took up her position with an arm around Mrs Mehta, Annie smiled at the woman guard, who this time responded.

"It's harder for some," she said.

Annie nodded, stroking Mrs Mehta's hair.

"She's not like the others we've got in here." The guard motioned with the back of her head in the general direction of everyone else. "Although there's a few like her at the moment. You get them after a crackdown."

"Do they stay long?"

The woman guard turned herself into a exclamation mark. "That's not for me to say!" Yet having expressed her surprise that she should have been asked such a thing, she offered an explanation.

"That's capital P politics. And capital L law. We're just prison officers." She made a bracket in the air with her hands. "Lower case." She tossed her short hair. "Lower case and lower caste."

Annie examined her more carefully. It was unusual for an Indian to speak openly about caste like that. For a government employee to defy official convention hinted at an independent personality. For a gaol guard to do so carried a whiff of insurrection.

She was a pleasant person in her mid-thirties, with a handsome, open face. She had embellished her khaki uniform, somehow creating the faint colour of a handkerchief's edge above her left breast pocket. She wore tiny pearl earrings and a gold bangle and her skirt was as short as it presumably could be and remain within the regulatory limit.

"Life can be rough sometimes," she said.

Annie sensed that this woman could be a friend, but the atmosphere of the gaol was so forbidding and so unfamiliar that she could be mistaken. She had to tread carefully. Anyway, Mrs Mehta had stopped crying.

"Can you cut up the mangoes yourself?"

"Oh, yes," the woman guard interrupted. "Politicals are allowed to have utensils."

"Well, then, that's something. You can have a feast tonight."

The look which Mrs Mehta directed at Annie was that of a person who never expected to enjoy food again. It was a look that acknowledged an unbridgeable gap between them, widening each time Annie raised their hopes, or her voice, in an effort to reach across the gap. Mrs Mehta looked forlornly at Annie as if she would be happier were the situation acknowledged by both of them to be hopeless.

"Have you heard anything of Professor Ganguly?" Annie asked casually.

Mention of the nimble, warm-hearted professor was another trigger of Mrs Mehta's bountiful store of tears. This time, the friendly guard took a couple of steps forward and with a formal hand resting lightly on one shoulder helped Annie to calm the weeping woman.

"Perhaps it is time for the interview to end," she suggested.

Annie looked at her watch. She was relieved to be given an excuse to leave. She had not learned anything useful from Mrs Mehta, but the guard's reference to "politicals" provided a clue. How quickly you turn away from a person when the spark of life has gone. How avidly you turn to a person when the spark of life is strong. Before she left, Annie asked the guard for her telephone number. "I'll also give you my mobile," the woman said. "Then you can catch me when I'm out and about." The way she said it, with a side glance and a teasing shake of her head, made being "out and about" seem highly adventurous.

Sitting in her thinking chair with the cat on her lap, Annie puzzled over Gopala's behaviour. When they met that first night, black and white, bound tight in their separate histories, they were as trustworthy as competitors meeting in a game for the first time. Now, there were intimacies, associations, responsibilities, rebuffs and misunderstandings, turning them into real people. Her false start at the bungalow, when she had presented herself with her luggage as a permanent guest, was not mentioned again, but she could not remove from her mind the impression that he had failed her. He had not even accompanied her to the hotel. When the chips were down, when she had turned to him, he had not been there. He was prepared to use her association with the authority of the residence to get himself out of trouble, but when that authority turned against her, he buckled.

The world outside, culture and religion, politics and history, was pressing down on her, and she wondered if her relationship with Gopala was strong enough to bear the weight. In an emergency you needed people you could trust, not just because they were clear-headed and knew what was what but because they were the same as you, thought the same, felt the same. She wasn't a flag-waver but at times like this you had to stop reaching out, stop trying to understand, and just be yourself, with people you could trust.

She remembered a childhood holiday, when they stayed in a caravan park on the Great Ocean Road. In the early morning she would lie awake and listen to the gentle breathing of the family. She would hear the first bird calls, the crunch and slither of the surf. Under the curtain drawn across the window above her bunk, she could, if she raised her head, catch a glimpse of light on the horizon between sea and sky. It was an exalted moment that always explained satisfactorily for her, if for no one else, why she should not take part in the activity that so closely followed. First were the "coo-ee" calls, then the rat-tat-tat on recalcitrant partitions, then entire families, including hers, would tumble out of bed for the Morning Walk, the only time her parents agreed to do anything together. Even as surprising, the boys followed them. They would return, bright-eyed and bushy-tailed, keen to explain in detail their slightest experience. If one of them had seen a rabbit or a wallaby, or noticed the sun rising from the sea (like a new coin, said one of the boys in bewildered wonder) or some strangely shaped driftwood or a piece of rock as smooth as a pebble from the turmoil of the water or just a dead fish on the beach, they would discuss it with a kind of innocence Annie could not bear. She knew it would wear off by breakfast, if not sooner. So she stayed in bed. They would find her reading, or just lying there with her eyes closed. She developed arguments in praise of idleness. She was at loggerheads with everyone until breakfast restored bickering to its central role in the family.

You needed familiar people, even when you took pains to remain apart from them.

She wondered whether she could experience India just sitting in her room. She could live happily at the hotel, letting India swirl around her. Those who wished to visit her could be given an appropriate time for an appointment, as if she were a dignitary or a doctor. She had grown up hating to be inside the house in Gardenvale. It was dark and dingy, shabby and smelly, full of noise and conflict. Outside was sunshine and fresh air, space and time, freedom. It was also banishment. "Go outside and play. Run around outside for a while. Stop moaning and go outside. Stop cluttering up the house and go outside. Outside! I'm cooking." But in India, outside was austere, even threatening. It needed to be experienced in carefully managed forays. It could be imagined best from inside, by someone observant and self-contained.

Like a cat. Its big, empty eyes, utterly unresponsive, were fixed on hers.

"Puss, puss," she said, holding out a hand. "Miaow, miaow."

The cat stood up, stretched every part of its body, wound its way over her shoulder to the window sill, its tail tickling her neck, and then jumped, landing on a bough of the tree.

Indians, Annie thought, are so deeply rooted in their own country, or their own bit of their country, that they cannot hope to explain themselves to foreigners. Their lives are beyond explanation, so deep are the roots, so complex the branches, so intricate the foliage. They were delighted, of course, to meet foreigners. All their best qualities, including their good looks, came to life in the presence of foreigners. They charmed them and even copied their ways, because foreigners represented freedom – and sometimes also power, such as an invitation to travel at some government's expense – but they did not want to know them well. They had enough worries and obligations of their own. When Indians were born, they were not born free. They were born entangled with family, community, country and the dreaded promise of reincarnation, that everything you did was calculated for and against your rebirth at a higher or lower level of consciousness.

She was sitting under the big tree, reading, when she shivered. The daylight hours were perceptibly cooler and at night the temperature dropped. She went to her room to fetch a pullover. It was then she saw the coat hanging behind the door.

Mrs Mehta must have put it there. It was a rough-surface cloth of a strange colour, a kind of purple brown, with flecks of green in a sort of pattern, but age had blurred everything into a dull violet when exposed to sunlight. Even so, it had a definite look, a presence, as if it knew it was waiting there to be claimed. She slipped it on. It was long, down to her calves, but the shoulders fitted. In the wardrobe mirror she looked like a hippie, or a waif. But she left it on. She wanted Mrs Mehta to see her in it. Also, she liked the texture. She ran her hands up and down the knobbly tweed, in and out of the silk pockets. But something was wrong. It looked too strong and heavy for her, propped in her basket-weave shoes. With a quick eye, she measured the distance between the floor and the bottom of the coat, her height and the width of her shoulders, the shape of her ankles. She needed something more solid on her feet. That was it!

She walked the streets of old Delhi before she found them. She wore the coat so that when she tried them on she could check how they looked. Also the colour. By the time she bought the boots, slim and shiny in brown leather, half-heeled with a thatched pattern on the outside, she had become a familiar figure on the streets of the old city. When she walked she could feel the hem of the coat swinging. She never went inside a shop. All their wares were displayed on the pavement. Spices, sweets (with accompanying wasps), clothes, brass, jewellery, marble tablets, even the latest electronics. Restaurants, vegetarian, non-vegetarian and what was called "pure vegetarian", served food on hot metal plates, parota, idly, poori potato. Pan sellers sat behind their desks with two stacks of leaves, the drawer of the desk containing coins for change mixed with single cigarettes. They applied a thick white paste with a stick. Then, depending on the order, they opened one of the cylindrical tins filled with powders and glass jars containing red cubes of jelly. Eight different kinds of bidis, four types of Western cigarettes. Some sold sachets of pan in many-flavoured combinations sealed in garish foil. Near the pan sellers were the tea sellers (chai wallahs) pumping gas to their flames while milk boiled and handfuls of sugar dissolved.

The human flow on the streets was so dense with energy and purpose yet so slow that Annie fully expected to see someone in a hurry walking on other people's shoulders, like a sheep dog. New Delhi had a suburban feeling, large old trees hanging over empty streets as wide as rivers and at its centre, rearing construction sites and swirling traffic. The old city had long ago choked itself into a state of stability; a vast traffic jam wound its way laboriously through the narrow streets, packed with cycle-rickshaws, auto-rickshaws, maxi-rickshaws (seating six to eight), even the occasional hand-pulled rickshaw, relic of colonial times which official India had tried to banish on the ground that it was offensive to human dignity. Motorbikes, cars, buses and trucks all nudged each other in the vain hope of speeding up the flow. Occasionally, one would break through in a momentary burst until blocked again by hunched men pushing long, flat wooden carts with two central wheels or by women carrying bundles of cloth or trays on their heads or by men carrying sacks of grain on their shoulders or by bullock-drawn carts.

Policemen, in khaki and moustache, directed the flow with imperious, impotent gestures. Sometimes they leaned, proud and bored, on their thick canes as the traffic ground to an actual halt and red streams of pan spittle splashed around them. Billboards and advertising were everywhere, in such a jumbled state that the impact of each message was lost, jostling for survival like everything else. However, on the back of an auto-rickshaw growling and throbbing in front of her, she read: "God is Globalisation".

It could be her imagination, but she was convinced there were fewer beggars in the old city, or perhaps just fewer children begging. She noticed children in India. At home, she was still living with the memory of her brothers and had put the thought of bearing children behind her, or so far ahead of her that it was out of mind, but she found herself bothered in India by the plight of poor children. She could not stand the sight of their thin, dirty bodies fighting in the gutter over a few coins tossed from the momentarily opened window of a waiting car.

She took off her sunglasses to examine a pavement stall of what appeared to be cashmere shawls. In New Delhi, around Connaught Circle or on the way to the library, she felt unprotected without her sunglasses, partly to shield the glare, partly to keep out pollution, like diesel fumes, flying splinters and grit, and partly to seal off her identity from the world. In the old city, she did not feel in need of protection. She felt strangely safe. She walked back to The Trilby with her sunnies perched on her head and a spring in her step.

"What is beauty?" she asked, looking in the mirror. She did not want to look the way other people looked. She wanted to look the way she was, herself. People dressed according to the role they thought they were performing, but the roles were written by the cockatoos. You can be this, they said, or perhaps, with luck and perseverance, you can be that. You look nice like this, they said, or that. If you do this or that, you will be rewarded, because others, who have power and influence, prefer people who do this or that. And who dress like people who do this or that.

She grinned at herself in the mirror. She put a cigarette in a corner of her mouth and put her hands in the coat pockets. She did not look like anyone else in the entire world, certainly not in India where women were either decorous in saris or, if defiantly young, flaunted bare midriffs above tight pants. Something else pleased her. She was covered almost completely from head to toe. Her body, whose secrets Gopala knew, was not for public display. The more intense her bodily pleasures became, the more secret they were.

She went to the rocking chair to think. A cat came. It wound its way along a bough of the big tree, slunk onto the window sill and seeing Annie, jumped on her lap. "Hello, cat," Annie said, stroking it forgetfully. It was a female, tabby, neatly marked, affectionate. It rubbed against Annie's hands, arms, breasts, neck, chin, cheeks, even her ears. It dug its claws into her skirt, kneaded and purred. She could sense the tension in its body as it pushed and prodded, nudged and nuzzled. She could feel bones as she stroked the curve of its back.

"Aren't they feeding you properly?" She took the cat in her hands, one hand under each shoulder blade, and wiggled its stretched-out paws against her nose, like powder pads. Perched on its hind legs, it observed her calmly through a tangle of forelimbs.

It would be wonderful to be a cat. No contribution to make to history and civilisation, no obligations and responsibilities to society, no huge superstructure of power and organisation pressing down on you, just sentient existence. Suddenly, she understood reincarnation perfectly. She peered intently into the cat's eyes.

"Who are you?" she inquired gently. The cat's eyes were alert and vacant at the same time. "How do you do?" said Annie, shaking one of its paws. The paw limply survived the transaction, and then returned to rest alongside the other on Annie's lap. "You! You!" she cried, nuzzling its nose.

Then, pushing away the cat, which landed neatly on the floor, she leaned out the window. Oh, to be a cat! Or a bird, flying higher and higher in the sky! Oh, to be a tree, rooted deeper and deeper in the ground, breathing in the sunlight, sending out shoots to touch the morning air. Or a flower bud, the tendril of a fern, a blade of grass. But flowers did not last, and the life of butterflies and ladybirds was short. She would not want to be a mouse, she thought, and certainly not a rat. Nor an ant, even with their work ethic. And even cats could not escape history. Were you an Indian cat, an Egyptian cat, a Mesopotamian cat or a Chinese cat? Or were you just a cat, the form of a cat?

What a complicated business reincarnation was. It wasn't just a choice of heaven or hell, or the final curtain of the non-believer, but endless recycling, past, present and future. Once you're on the wheel of life, you never get off. She returned to the rocking chair and fixed the cat with an unfriendly, unforgiving gaze.

What Annie did not know was that Pat had reacted to her departure from the residence with uncharacteristic venom. He had left the breakfast table after their discussion with a vague sense that despite her belligerence she would, when she had had time to consider all the implications, settle down. Settling down was high on Pat's list of virtues. The art of diplomacy was persuading people to settle down, although diplomats represented governments with all sorts of urgent and intractable problems and were convinced that other governments were set upon making the situation worse. If governments, convinced of their sovereign right to be independent, could be persuaded to settle down, surely Annie, a sensible girl, would do the same once she examined the practical side of things. Accepting the practical side of things was also high on Pat's list – and it worked both ways. He accepted that if Annie wished to continue to see this fellow, there was nothing he or Iris could do about it, but there was a difference between doing it discreetly and flaunting it. Visiting Gopala's bungalow in broad daylight was asking for trouble.

So when Annie walked out without a word of where she was going, he was annoyed.

It was not a moral issue, he convinced himself, and certainly not racial, even if living in colour-conscious India it was difficult not to be affected. It was simply that he felt responsible for Annie, the daughter of a family friend, and he expected her to show some respect for his – and Iris's – position. When he was told by Mr Gleeson that she had taken a taxi with her luggage to Gopala's bungalow, he decided that her behaviour released him from the undertaking he had given not to punish Gopala. The undertaking had been made in respect of petrol theft, but Gopala had crossed a more important line. All local employees at the Australian high commission knew the line existed, even if it wasn't in any book of rules. He had taken advantage of Annie, a young Australian woman with a spirit of adventure on her first visit to India. Pat wondered how they had met, presumably on the compound while Gopala was on duty. That was bad enough, but Annie was also a guest at the official residence. Gopala was not only breaking the rules, he was defying the High Commissioner. He had to be sent packing, or the infection would spread.

Pat instructed Mr Gleeson to sack Gopala, as quickly and as painfully, in a material sense, as possible without breaking any laws. Officially, he would be sacked for stealing petrol. His corroborating witness had disappeared, so that was that. Mr Gleeson did not need to have the i's dotted and the t's crossed. This was the kind of assignment he enjoyed, being able to squeeze every drop of personal satisfaction from it without having to bear any responsibility for it. To any injured inquiry he could simply retort, "Ask the High Commissioner."

Decisive in the turn of events, none of this was known to Annie. What Pat did not know was that Gopala, anticipating retaliation from Pat if Annie stayed at the bungalow, had despatched her to Mrs Mehta's hotel. Gopala had told Gleeson, during a heated exchange over his dismissal notice, but Gleeson had not considered the fact relevant to the crime of theft, which was established, and not wishing to muddy the waters of a nice, clean administrative procedure, did not tell the High Commissioner.

He mentioned it, however, to the police, because he knew they kept an eye on Mrs Mehta, and her friend, Professor Ganguly, who were members of a group practising eurhythmics, which the police suspected was a cover for other activities.

None of them knew that Gopala, angry and desolate at the loss of his job and his bungalow, encouraged to strike a blow for India against internal weaknesses and foreign influences, had concocted a bizarre form of retaliation. He would arrange for Annie to be kidnapped.

13

AT 2.14 AM SHE WAS wakened by loud knocking on her door. She glanced at her watch as she woke in fright and responding to one of those comic, practical impulses that come in a rush at times of crisis, urged herself to remember the exact time. She was still in bed when the door opened and two men entered. They turned on the light and standing with their backs to the open doorway asked her politely to come with them.

"If you please, ma'am."

She sat up in bed and stared blankly at them.

They were dressed in dark suits, white shirts and ties so indistinct in colour that they appeared to be the same. They were the same height and the same build. Even their faces were similar, young and smooth, with regular features and close-cropped hair. They looked official, which reassured her momentarily. They shifted their feet as her stare became indignant.

"What do you mean by breaking into my room?"

"We are here under emergency regulations to escort you to the police station," one of them recited. He rattled off the sub-section of a law.

"Who are you?"

"We are under instructions to take you to the police station."

"What for, for heaven's sake!"

"Our duty is to escort you safely to the police station. When you are there you will be told ... why we have brought you to the police station."

She was now scornful as well as indignant. "They should teach you logic before they send you out into the world. Why break into my room? To take you to the police station! Why take me to the police station? So that when we get there we can tell you why we broke into your room!"

Her mimicry made her respondent sound half-witted. Both of them. They grinned uneasily, but the one who had already spoken stuck to his guns.

"Would madam like to dress or should we take you the way you are?"

"You've made a mistake," she protested. "You've come to the wrong street or the wrong room at the wrong hotel."

A woman, or for that matter a man, sitting up in bed in the middle of the night confronted by intruders who stand in the doorway with their arms crossed and their eyes hard and empty, is not in a strong bargaining position. She was going to be taken somewhere. That was certain. She gave up and got out of bed, adopting a haughty stance, hand on hip. Unmoved, silent, they observed her with flat, evaluating eyes as if she were performing an indecent act on stage.

"I can see that you have neither the authority nor the wit to change course. The only question is whether you are going to watch me get dressed."

They turned their backs obligingly. Over jeans and blouse she put on the tweed coat and pulled on her new boots. She decided not to bother with make-up or cleaning her teeth; she would not be long. She swung a bag over one shoulder.

"Let's go, numbskulls!"

They followed her down the passage. She expected slits of light, muffled voices, peeping eyes, but the doors remained closed, the rooms behind them quiet. The small hotel was still and silent.

As they approached the reception desk, one of the generals stood up. Annie confronted him. "What kind of hotel is this?" she demanded. He lowered his eyes. "I'll have something to say to you later about strange men breaking into my room in the middle of the night." He wobbled his head in the manner of Gopala, shading good and evil into each other. She flicked a hand at him in exasperation, turned to the grinning duo behind her and marched through the foyer ahead of them. A small group of ragged bystanders watched from a distance outside as they whisked through the front doors to a waiting car.

The car, not big to begin with, was already half full. Two people were jammed in the front seat against the driver, their bodies side-on, their arms around each other's shoulders. Annie and her escorts squeezed into the back seat. She sat hunched forward in the middle, bundled up in the tweed coat, her bag on her knees.

The little black car jumped into action, nosing its way in low gear around the circular drive. She could see tentacles of bougainvillea against the sky. The car ventured in fits and starts into the wide, dark street. She became aware of the smell of human bodies, not unpleasant but potent. She was suddenly frightened. She should have rung Pat. She should have refused to leave the hotel until he or someone from the high commission arrived. If necessary, he would have accompanied her to the police station. Why did she do these things, these defiant, impulsive things that always got her into trouble?

It was dark outside and the neighbourhood in any case was unfamiliar. She had no idea where they were or where they were going.

"This is the way to the police station?"

"Yes, this is the way."

The voice was in the front but she was not sure from which of the three heads it came. Possibly the smallest, the low one in the middle. It looked more authoritative than the driver's, which was thrust forward on shoulders hunched over the wheel, or the big one on the far side, which was encased in a knitted cap.

Her escorts, impassive, stared ahead, their arms folded, their bodies tense and erect, avoiding contact with hers.

"Can anyone explain to me what this farce is all about?"

Yes, it was the little one in the middle. He turned his head slightly to acknowledge her presence as he spoke. "All in good time, memsahib."

"Don't memsahib me," Annie retorted. "Someone, and it could be you, is going to get a hell of a shock at the end of all this." She sliced her hand against her throat to signal the dire consequences. "Kaput!" In the circumstances, her graphic demonstration was unfortunate. She meant the end of someone's career, not their life. Thankful for the darkness, she made amends. "Someone's job will be on the line."

"We have orders," said Little Head.

The quality of the silence was as dense as the darkness. She could sense hostility, not to her but among the men in the car. They must be asking themselves, she told herself, why it took five men to escort a woman to a police station, why they had to burst into her room in the middle of the night, why they were all squashed into this little car. Perhaps they were also sensitive to the smell of human bodies. She was sitting so far forward that with only a small additional movement she would have been able to sniff Little Head's hair.

They were proceeding in what seemed like a semi-circular direction. The car veered persistently to the driver's side, although from time to time he jerked the steering wheel to make a correction in the other direction. The road was so wide and dark, with the lights of the car flicking and flashing up and down over bumps and sweeping around as the driver swerved to avoid obstacles, that it seemed like a deserted racetrack or a runway. It was a runway! She saw a parked aircraft.

"What are we doing at an airport?"

"All in good time, madam."

They were deporting her. Or taking her tortured body in a helicopter to dump it out at sea! She needed to do something. Anything! She leaned across the escort on her left, digging one elbow into a hefty thigh, and grabbed at the door. Her hand found and twisted a handle and the door flew open. There was a rush of cool air and a hissing of tyres. She struggled to throw herself from the car, but the escort blocked her by simply lying back and raising his buttocks and legs.

The small black car stopped abruptly. The open door sagged for a moment while she flailed and floundered without effect. Then it snapped shut and the car resumed its journey.

"We'll soon be there," said Little Head, with insolent indifference.

Unless the God she had long discarded decided for his own mysterious reasons that she was to be saved and struck her captors dead, she could do nothing to prevent Little Head from being right. She should keep her thoughts and her strength for the struggle that would come. She must remember: not a word to anyone until she had spoken to Pat.

They pulled up alongside a tin shed, blazing with light. The five men unloaded themselves and sauntered about, stretching, leaving Annie fuming in the middle of the back seat. If she was to be treated badly, as she evidently was, the least they could do was to acknowledge that she was an important person to be treated badly, not some nondescript passenger who could be left unattended in the back seat. She sat tight.

Little Head approached the open door and motioned her to leave the car. She remained unmoved, eyes straight ahead, knees up and close together.

"Would you prefer to be lifted out, madam?"

"I would prefer to be treated like a human being."

Little Head put one foot on an invisible running board and offered Annie an open hand. "Your obedient servant, ma'am."

Annie gathered herself together and eased herself from the car, ignoring his hand. Bulky in the tweed coat and the shoulder bag, she took time to extricate herself. As soon as she was standing erect her two escorts moved in, taking an elbow each, and shuffled her through an open, floodlit door. Inside, men were busy moving furniture, as if preparing a change of scene.

"This is not a police station," Annie announced, breaking their grip on her arms. She stood firmly in the middle of the hut, surrounded by removalists. "I demand to speak to the person in charge."

While the escorts conferred in murmurs, Little Head presented himself.

"I apologise for the mess. You will appreciate that our resources are under strain at the moment. Severe strain, in fact. All our police stations are full. Chock-a-block."

He smiled formally, acknowledging a shortcoming. "We're doing the best we can with makeshift places like this. As you can see, we use screens to give as much privacy as possible. People are coming and going all the time."

He tidied the cushions on a subsiding couch and motioned her to it, as if she were being asked to wait at an airport VIP lounge. She remained standing in the middle of the untidy floor.

"Why do you break into my room at 2.14 am and arrest me?"

"You are not under arrest, madam."

"Then what am I doing in this godforsaken place in the middle of the night?"

"You must not think that because you are here, it follows that Government of India holds anything against you. It does not necessarily follow at all."

"You could have fooled me."

"Not at all," he reasserted, soothingly. "You are here just for questioning."

"What if I don't want to be questioned? What if I just want to go back to my hotel and get into my bed? What if I sue you for disturbing my sleep? What if the hotel sues you for breaking and entering?"

He shook his head. "Those things do not happen in India. The Indian people understand that at times of emergency certain actions have to be taken. They are familiar with what is necessary when their country is facing a crisis."

In any case, the responsibility was not entirely on one side. "They knocked on the door, but you were sleeping so soundly." His tone of voice changed, now directed at an indulgent child, understandably ignorant of India's great troubles. "They were very keen not to miss you." He made the goons seem like anxious admirers.

Annie decided to examine Little Head more carefully. Standing on his own, away from Broad Shoulders and Beetling Brows, his head was not so little, perhaps merely normal. He was dressed in a Nehru jacket, open at the neck and without sleeves so that his white shirt ballooned down his arms. His baggy grey trousers and brown leather sandals gave him a casual, leisurely look.

She filed him away as small and spritely, with a twinkle in his eye.

"Please sit down for a moment."

"I prefer to stand."

"But we only draw attention to ourselves standing up and shouting. We can discuss these matters much more agreeably sitting down and talking quietly."

"Agreeably? What kind of language is that?"

"I'm sorry, I don't follow."

"Never mind. Are you the person in charge?"

"In a manner of speaking."

"Well, in a manner of speaking, I wish to make a telephone call before I sit down or say anything to you or anyone else."

"A telephone call?" He looked hopefully around the room. "I'm not sure that the telephone is connected." He examined a piece of equipment on a table. "No, it is not yet connected."

"There must be a telephone. This is an airport, isn't it?"

"In a manner of speaking, it is an airport. But this is a makeshift office and the telephone has not yet been connected, I am sorry to say. I do not know where the nearest telephone is."

His face drooped. He was sad having to acknowledge another shortcoming, but he quickly perked up. "You have your mobile perhaps?"

That question again. She had become so sensitive about eavesdropping that she had almost stopped using it. But she had made sure she had it this time, secure in the bag she was holding in her hands.

"Let me assure you, madam, that if the intention of your telephone call is to tell someone that you have been arrested and need to be represented here by a lawyer or an official from your embassy, there is no need. As I told you, you have not been arrested. You are here simply because we believe you may have information which is of interest to Government of India. All we ask is that we sit down quietly together and discuss some matters that are pertinent to the national emergency that has unfortunately ..."

He tailed off, leaving her wondering about the nature of the emergency. Had it occurred of its own volition, descending on everyone from on high, or had it simply been announced by someone, so that it was being made up by many Small-and-Spritelys as they went along. It could be interesting to discover what it was that "Government of India" wanted to talk about with her. She might find out why Mrs Mehta was in gaol. But she could not forget the two boyos who had broken into her room. It was not just their look-alike presence. Their docility scared her. They were so well-trained that they would do anything, anything at all, and then clean up the mess thoroughly afterwards. It flashed through her mind that they dealt with people as farmers handle animals. Their ruthlessness was so detached it seemed tinged with kindness.

"Until I have telephoned, I do not propose to say anything to anyone."

"May I offer a compromise," said Small-and-Spritely. "We will sit down and I will explain why you are here. You don't have to say anything. You only have to listen."

It seemed safe. She had nothing to lose. She sat on an arm of the couch. He took his place at the other end, opening a manila folder on his knees. "Well," he remarked, apparently pleased. "Here we are."

She waited without hope. She foresaw a lengthy dissertation broken by wisps of self-importance. He had a piquant smile. She could see his even, white teeth flashing with personal, perceptive asides, little pats on the back. At the end, she would still have to make up her own mind why she was wherever she was. However, Small-and-Spritely was determined to keep his side of the bargain, which was to talk. And she was heartened by his lack of interest in her mobile microphone, unlike Pat and Gopala. Perhaps he was just an honest cop.

"I can understand that for someone like yourself, coming from a country that is politically stable, even, some might say, placid, what is happening here comes as a shock. We are not a conspicuously law-abiding country unfortunately and there are forces at work intent upon undermining the progress we have made since independence. However, I would like to put you at your ease. Nothing is happening. Rather, of course something is happening, but it is nothing about which to be alarmed."

He was a doctor informing a patient that, despite impaired capability, she could expect to live a normal life, provided she followed instructions.

"You have eaten tandoori? All over the world people think this is an Indian dish, but it comes really from Pakistan and was not common in India until after partition."

Small-and-Spritely faded as the threatening presence of officialdom and became yet another Indian with an inferiority complex.

"Really."

"The British were very clever. They ruled through the Indian princes but they used the Muslims for their own purposes, against the Indian people."

Where had she heard that before? She examined the buttons on the old tweed coat, wrapped it more tightly around her and waited.

"The old city is predominantly Muslim." His quick eyes darted at her. "The emergency is everywhere, but it is also in the old city of Delhi in the very particularity of this place."

"I'm so glad we weren't forgotten." Her head-toss passed unnoticed.

"Forgotten? This is the centre."

"Of what?"

"Of India! This is the national capital." He smiled benignly at her ignorance. "We are in the eye of the storm. You know that in a storm the centre is the steadiest, calmest point. Everything is under control here, law and order prevails. But outside, beyond the national capital, the fate of India is in the balance."

An image formed in Annie's head like a crude cartoon, showing a set of scales with the continent of India lolling on one side and herself, sitting in Buddha-style on crossed legs and with open palm upheld, on the other. The scales tipped down steeply on the side of India, as passive as a lump of concrete, while her side, despite her best efforts to summon gravity and weight, rose higher and higher.

She felt light-headed. "If I jump off, will the fate of India be decided?"

"Jump off? What is this jump off? You are a guest of Government of India, sitting quietly on this ... comfortable sofa." He touched it. "You have a sense of humour, madam. That is a valuable thing. Life is full of sorrow." He examined her with mounting admiration. "It is necessary to laugh at life sometimes, in order to keep a balance. Yes, you have a good sense of humour."

He checked himself with a new thought.

"Like the British. They prided themselves on their sense of humour. They thought Indians were lacking in humour. They thought we took ourselves too seriously. They were mistaken, of course. Indians have a very fine sense of humour. Not that we do not take ourselves seriously. We certainly do take ourselves seriously. Since independence, India has had to take its role in world affairs very seriously indeed. But we have an excellent sense of humour. Excellent."

She waited for examples, hoping for free entertainment, but he continued in the same expository vein for some time. Then, suddenly, his manner changed and he asked the first of the questions she had been brought from her room at the small hotel to answer.

"What, in your opinion, is the nature of the relationship between Mrs Mehta and Professor J.P. Ganguly?"

Later, wrapped in the old tweed coat and curled up unhappily on the back seat, she experienced waves of luxurious solitude and sharp crosswinds of anxiety in the warmth and darkness of the little car. She could not explain, even to herself, how it happened, how, after all, she did not refuse to answer questions until she had spoken to Pat.

With its light load, the little black car bounced and swerved on the wide, dark road even more noticeably than before. The driver, hunched over the wheel, muttered curses as the headlights picked up obstacles, jerking the vehicle to avoid them, grinding the gears to reduce speed, all oblivious to passenger comfort in the back seat.

It had been as clear as crystal – not a word from her until her rights were established, until she knew why she was being dragged from her bed in the middle of the night like a common criminal, until it was clear what, if anything, she was accused of having done. But somehow, when the questioning actually began, it was different. You could think like that before, but when you found yourself in an actual situation, in a real place with real people, the clear lines of argument you had prepared in your head began to wobble. The reality of the present took over, and you just accepted it. Everything was so confusing, anyway, what was the point in trying to be clear-headed and purposeful?

She defends herself. She is not weak. She kept the cockatoos at bay. She stood up to the execrable Gleeson. She walked out on Pat and Iris rather than accept their hospitality on terms that infringed her rights as a person. And it was obvious that while the boyos were crude and possibly brutal and would deliver her inert to a distant ditch if they thought that was what they were asked to do, Small-and-Spritely was a sensitive, intelligent person, not wanting to harm her, wanting, rather, to return her unharmed as soon as he could to the small hotel. It was in her interest to strengthen his position, not theirs. When you thought about it, her behaviour was sensible and rational.

In any case, how could she be expected to understand all the ins-and-outs of Indian politics, not to mention the labyrinth of the Indian legal system and its enforcement agencies? Who gave the boyos their instructions? Was Small-and-Spritely really in charge? To whom was he responsible? Or was it more likely, as she suspected, that the whole show was a disorganised mess? No one was actually in charge and anything might happen. If this were the case, she needed to be cooperative when she was dealing with a sensible, civilised person.

Anyway, she had answered the questions. Perhaps she should have been more careful, but she was grappling with something deeper than this silly little plot they were avid about, whatever it was. She had tried to explain to Small-and-Spritely that she had only talked to the professor once, although she had noticed him flitting in and out of the small hotel. But Small-and-Spritely was insistent. He wanted to know exactly what Professor Ganguly had said when the three of them had taken afternoon tea together.

She could not remember. All she could remember was an avalanche of words. And his enthusiasm for certain trees.

"Trees?"

Small-and-Spritely was highly suspicious of the professor's interest in trees and wanted to know precisely which ones he liked, and why, but Annie could not remember the botanical names. All she was certain of, because she had noticed it at the time, was that he was affected by scent. She mentioned his fondness for the sandalwood tree.

"Sandalwood!"

Small-and-Spritely scribbled away as if he was finding it difficult to contain himself, knowing that Professor J.P. Ganguly was fond of sandalwood. Turning to another sheet of paper, he ticked off items from what looked like a list. Then he turned his attention to a matter that seemed to intrigue him, because he made several attempts to begin, screwing up his face with intense concentration, before asking the question that he seemed always to have somewhere in his mind, pressing to get out.

"What, in your opinion, is the nature of the relationship between Mrs Mehta and Professor J.P. Ganguly?"

"Relationship?"

"Would you say the professor and Mrs Mehta are friends, or more than friends?"

"They are certainly friends."

"Good friends?"

"Yes."

"Very good friends?"

"If you're really asking me whether they are lovers, I have no idea. And, if I did, the last person I would tell would be you."

He showed his sensitivity by sitting quietly for some time, eyes lowered. He straightened his shoulders as if pulling himself together in the line of duty.

"I would not embarrass you, madam, by asking anything so personal. Lovers, that is something else." He seemed, however, lost for a while in what "something else" might be. "No, I am interested in another matter. Are they business partners, perhaps? Or would you say they are political associates?"

Annie knew (in her bones) that something substantial existed between Professor Ganguly and Mrs Mehta, but she did not know what it was. It was either deeply and confidently intimate, so that they knew in public exactly how to behave without betraying each other, or it existed in such an unusual form that it did not conform to any known rules. Sometimes their easy and pleasurable acceptance of each other seemed telepathic.

"They are kindred spirits. Soul mates."

"Soul mates!"

Small-and-Spritely chuckled. It was a clean, uncomplicated chuckle, reminding her of the Man from Bangalore. The thought that Professor Ganguly and Mrs Mehta had a spiritual relationship amused him.

"I will be frank with you, madam. Whatever else, they are not soul mates."

"Well, if you know so much, why do you bother asking me?"

"Ah, yes. A good question. It is perhaps time to move on."

"More than time, I'd say."

"Indeed. Allow me to move forward another step. What do you know of the so-called study group – Mrs Mehta's husband, Professor Ganguly, Mr Damodar and others?"

"I don't know about any group. Studying what?"

"Well, they study the stars." By raising his eyes, Small-and-Spritely assumed an expression of infinite disbelief. He seemed embarrassed. "They do eurhythmics."

"All those men, dancing," exclaimed Annie, pleased to be confronted with something tangible.

"It's not dancing." He weaved his hands and wiggled his body. "It's interpreting the harmony of music with bodily movements. Harmony comes from the outside – and also from the inside. There is the music, but there is also a feeling of trust in responding to the music. You trust the music and you trust other members of the group. When trust breaks down, the group ... breaks up." He smiled at his verbal facility. "Which is what happened, apparently, in this case. But you know nothing of this group?"

"Nothing," said Annie.

"What in your opinion is the relationship between Mrs Mehta and Mr Damodar?"

"Who?"

"Mr Gopala Damodar."

Annie had been waiting for that question from the moment she first entered the little black car, without being consciously aware that she was. It was a question that had been hovering in her own mind as far back as the first night at the small hotel, when she had realised that it was not Gopala's kind of hotel. She had expected to find the bare bones of Indian-style accommodation, inefficient and uncomfortable, when she had travelled to old Delhi on his recommendation that night and instead had found herself ensconced in comfort, with a clientele as decorous and thoughtful as members of an ashram.

Mrs Mehta was not Gopala's kind of Indian. She was Iris's kind of Indian, or Pat's, or Killarney Cottage's kind of Indian.

"How, when you moved from the residence, dear lady, did you happen to come to Mrs Mehta's ... establishment?"

She told him. She told him about Gopala, about the row with Gleeson over the petrol, about the showdown with Iris and Pat. Released at last to speak, she spoke without interruption as these matters floated to the surface of her mind. She described her surprise at finding the small hotel so comfortable, how she knew as soon as she saw it that Gopala could not have thought of it himself. She described the interior of his bungalow. She spoke of his poetry and even remembered some of his father's maxims. She provided social background on Iris, explaining, however, that her taste now was impeccable. She expressed the view that Mrs Mehta had a talent for organisation and that her large staff was almost militarily efficient. But mostly she just wanted to talk about her relationship with Gopala.

Small-and-Spritely scribbled, head down, like a reporter suddenly provided with a story for which he had been waiting all his working life. What exploded in his surprised face was her determination to expose her relationship with Gopala the way it really was. She wanted to let it all come out, because it was a relief to be able to talk to someone else about Gopala and also because ... she knew that what she told Small-and-Spritely would go into the system with a degree of accuracy. She wanted them all to know the truth, the whole truth and nothing but the truth.

Let it all hang out. Shove it up them!

She wanted them to know what had actually happened, even how she and Gopala had met at the pond in the darkness of the garden. She wanted to convey to them the pain and the ecstasy, the sweet flesh, the hard power and the high ridge. She wanted to cut through their stratagems, their equivocations and niceties, their unfathomable prejudices. Let them bother with the consequences, whatever they were. Let them work out what it meant for stability or security, or "Government of India", or for that matter civilisation, when a black man wanted a white woman because she was white and the white woman wanted the black man because he was black. It was their problem, not hers. Let them worry about the consequences if the black man and the white women discovered in their exhilaration some affection for each other, a certain tenderness. She had had the experience. She knew what it was like. No one could take it away from her, whatever they chose to think about it.

Let the chips fall where they may. She remembered from somewhere: "The truth shall set you free."

That was what she was trying to say when she had answered Small-and-Spritely's questions. All the rest was their problem. Now, tired and uneasy, battling the crosswinds of guilt with closed eyes as the little car swerved and bounced its way home, she wondered if she should, after all, ring Pat. But she still didn't know why she had been hauled to a makeshift police station in the middle of the night and she did not want to have to go through it all again with Pat, explaining her answers. She felt guilty because she had not discovered why Mrs Mehta was in gaol, although it was obvious that Small-

and-Spritely thought she and Ganguly were up to no good. Should she try to find the professor? He would sit there, his face shining over his bow tie, and rattle on as if he had just been wound up, without answering any of her questions, if she could think of the right questions to ask. And what of Gopala? Where did he fit in? Where was he?

It was all too much. Tired, guilty, confused and vaguely fearful, she decided to turn her back on it and walk off. Give it away.

She rolled the phrase over her tongue and through her head and was comforted by it. Giving it away wasn't the same as giving up. Giving up was an act of desperation, involving an attitude to life and personal responsibility. Giving it away had a certain charm, a hint of self-regard; it could be a moral act, relinquishing something that was not good for you in the first place.

She would give it away, the whole box and dice, Gopala, Pat and Iris, Mrs Mehta, the small hotel, Professor Ganguly, the Man from Bangalore, the library, the Aryans, Harappan civilisation, the woman guard at the gaol, Lodi Gardens, despicable Gleeson, Mussoorie, the maharaja and the maharani, the pond, Radha and Krishna, the Bhagavad Gita, the Mahabharata, Bollywood, the bomb, the purple coat, the cat. The whole Indian box and dice.

She would go back to Gardenvale and settle down. She laughed out loud with relief at the incredulity of what she was proposing.

Her mother is standing by the sink, her face flushed, a tea towel over her shoulder. She thrusts the towel at Annie, who comes up to her waist, and stalks from the kitchen. Annie can see only the tops of the pile of dishes in the sink, so she finds a stool and stands on it, placing the towel over her shoulder, like her mother, with a slap of defiance. Then she takes each dish from the sink and smashes it on the floor. As she raises each dish and throws it down, her face at first flashes with anger, but it takes some time to smash all the dishes so she adopts a look of grim determination to accompany a slow-burning fuse of purposeful action.

She acknowledges that when the smashed plates are uncovered a century later no one will take them to be anything other than smashed plates. Digging up history was hard work in Australia, like everything else, but it wasn't a confidence trick. When you found a spoon someone had once used you didn't think you had discovered the secret of life.

She wants to live normally again, catch a tram, buy an ice cream. She wants to be herself, not reaching out, not worrying whether she has said or done the right thing. She isn't blaming anyone; it's her fault, not India's. She's the one that jumped in at the deep end and has been flailing about ever since, but she feels a certain pleasure in her renunciation, her rejection of the India project. Too many gods. Too complex and splendid a culture, too huge a history. She wants to get back to the boring sanity of Australia, away from magic and mystery, back to the eternal debate about which political party is prepared to spend more on education and health, or on defence and espionage, back to the sad acceptance that life has no meaning except its trivial pursuits, like football and the poker machines, that people don't really know what their destiny is, and don't care, that God never presided over the birth of this nation, nor cares now about its future, that liberty, equality and fraternity are hard-won social, political and economic benchmarks, not emblematic fashion statements. Back to the humdrum labour of getting by.

As soon as she gets to the hotel she will ring the flying kangaroo and get the earliest flight to Melbourne. She won't leave a note at Gopala's bungalow, she won't telephone Iris or Pat (she will write Iris a vaguely apologetic letter), she won't tell any of Mrs Mehta's generals until she checks out at the front desk (when she will give them a piece of her mind about the invasion of her privacy). Just pack up and go. Turn her back on it and walk. Give it away!

When they reach the small hotel, the driver remains seated, shoulders over the wheel, the engine revving. She opens the same door she had forced open earlier and swivels herself out.

"Goodnight," she says primly.

It is early morning. The sun is rising, red and throbbing. She looks for the blue of the bougainvillea tentacles that had reached into the night sky when she had left. She wants to stand still for a moment and become enveloped in the world as night becomes day. She wants every moment of the rest of her time in India to be memorable.

The Last Kiss

But this is not her hotel. This is a derelict house in a deserted, dusty garden. Hooded figures move rapidly towards her. They surround her, stiff-arm and push her through a collapsing doorway into a room of total darkness, smelling of sour milk or perhaps bats. They take her shoulder bag, empty her pockets, force down her shoulders until she squats on the floor with her back against a pole. Quickly and seemingly expertly, they run a chain several times around her body and secure it to the pole. She hears the click as a padlock closes. Then they leave the room, the last one dragging the door shut.

14

"THE IMAGINATIVE MIND IS THE curse of the incarcerated body."

She had read it somewhere. The way to survive behind bars is to have a routine, do the same things, think the same thoughts, hold on to what you know, anything to reassure yourself that you are still in control. Don't let your mind roam, don't speculate, don't for a moment consider the possibility that you have lost control of your life, which you have.

She had read it in the comfort of her own country, probably in one of the magazines that came with the weekend newspapers, some local person trapped in some strange land, or a foreign political figure or intellectual dissident talking about their past, selling their memoirs. She had enjoyed the irony, the conscious will to counter the rational mind, and had not thought she would ever need it.

So what should she think, over and over again? It would be dangerous to relive the moments with Gopala on the big teak bed. Even brushing them aside made her tremble. She could see the muscles of his shoulders pushing out the stiff creases in his ironed shirt. She pushed away his sad, brilliant smile. In came Professor Ganguly like a dancing bear, his eyes cannoning off each other over his bow tie. When she brushed him away, Mrs Mehta entered, sobbing, with a prison guard holding her up.

She tried Gardenvale and the dishes and was assailed by the memory of burned apricots. Her mother stewed apricots in the largest saucepan, doused with nutmeg and two quarters of a lemon. She was always busy with other domestic chores, allowing the apricots to boil over, creating an aroma that wafted through the house. The family would converge on the kitchen, sniffing the air. The smell of burned apricots, Annie remembered, was irresistible, like toast and coffee.

Her mind wandered, looking at real estate in nearby Elsternwick. Real estate was an interesting, safe topic. Once, on a flight to Sydney, she had read an article on "cosmopolitan" Elsternwick in an in-flight magazine and had considered moving there; better than down-market Bentleigh or up-market Caulfield. Elsternwick had always had good restaurants because of its Jewish population, especially from Hungary, and now it was multicultural because of Asians, especially Chinese. It had a sensible core of hard-working, family-centred life, yet wasn't suburban. She could even envisage a Federation house, with a gargoyle on the roof and a picket fence.

But anger resurfaced, like an old cough. Why was she still living with her parents? Cheap and easy, that was the answer. The boys had gone and her parents barely spoke to each other, or to her, so she came and went like a boarder, with her own entrance through the laundry at the back. She had put so much of her life into her studies that when they were over she found she had lost the knack of connecting with the world outside. It was easier to stay at home and continue living in her head. But it was ridiculous, still living with her parents. It had kept her out of trouble in her teens but now it was stopping her having a life of her own. She must get out of her parents' house, establish her own circle. Then she was overwhelmed by the fear that she might never see home again.

Summoning Pat and Iris had the same effect, irritation, and then a surge of nostalgia. Melbourne. All those streets of shops, the discounts, the summer sales, how did they make a living? It was like that all over the world, buying and selling, but Melbourne was different, you didn't expect it, the people weren't really slick or desperate enough, or tricky. Really? What about the gangster killings and corrupt police? And the brothels and all-night dives and topless barmaids and pole dancers and pokies and the Casino? And the rich suburbs, with their tree-lined streets and hidden garages, and the poor suburbs, with their broken footpaths and trucks parked in driveways. Melbourne was as good and bad as anywhere.

But it had a good network of bicycle paths. Something Iris Murdoch had written about the bicycle being the perfect human vehicle drifted into her memory, but she could not remember the exact wording to repeat over and over again.

She wondered if methodically devising a site at Harappa for her project might work, but then argued with herself whether the Indus Valley civilisation was or was not Aryan, with a vivid interjection from the Man from Bangalore. "Never the twain shall meet ... You have seen the marriage columns in the newspapers, high caste boy, fair girl ... the light Aryan north and the dark Dravidian south." So what about the Man from Bangalore himself? He was reassuring, a calm redoubt in a chaotic world; she could dwell on him without getting upset. But she hardly knew him and Bangalore housed not only India's information industry, but also its nuclear secrets. In a flash of fevered imagination, the Moghul tombs floated down from outer space to land in the Lodi Gardens like nuclear-armed flying saucers.

So she recited her school anthem, which was in Latin. In her head, over and over again.

"Nostra schola, te amamus/ O sodales, concinamus." Over and over again. "Nostra schola, schola alma/ Semper gloriam petamus!"

The door scraped open and a shrouded figure scuttled in on bare feet. It squatted by her side, jingled the padlock, pulled on the chain and then settled down, like a garden gnome, as if for a long stay. She discovered her voice, which she had been hearing but not using.

"What do you want?" she croaked. She sounded fierce.

"Money," the voice said.

So that was it. She was a hostage, being held by some ramshackle bunch for what they probably thought would be a huge ransom. She could hear the man's heavy breathing under his hood. How much? She needed someone to tell her what the going rate was.

"Who are you?"

"Money," the voice said.

She was exhausted and scared, but this was like having a conversation with a poker machine. A one-word bandit. She giggled. She must take a grip on herself. She tried again.

"How much?"

"Money."

He stood up and shuffled off, dragging the door clumsily shut. Well, that was mercifully short, if not sweet. No doubt about his intentions. She tried to imagine what the conversation might have been like had it progressed. How much did they want? She hadn't taken much notice of currency values, hadn't the faintest idea how rescues like hers were arranged. One thing was for sure this time: Pat would be involved.

She went back to her school anthem, singing it this time not just in her head but in her actual voice, softly, over and over again, varying the presentation, now a Bach oratorio, now a Brahms lullaby. Listening to her voice, she discovered emotional depths in it, also a harsh sweetness that was intriguing, so she tested herself with some Auvergne folk songs. Then Enya, but her tone was either too light or too melancholy. Then Sade, but she could not be sultry. The effort made her sleepy. She had no idea what time of the day or night it was. She slept with her back against the pole, her head on her chest.

She was wakened by pressure from a plump, soft hand on her shoulder. The voice was lighter, clearer than the one before.

"You are hostage," it said. "You understand?"

She nodded.

"You understand you are hostage?"

"Yes."

"You are hostage because our brothers are in prison. Government of India put our brothers in prison. So you are hostage."

There was a lilt in his voice. She liked the way he arranged his sentences. His face was hidden in a cowl.

"Why me?" She cleared a husky throat. "I don't know anything about your brothers."

"You are tourist, spending hard currency which Government of India wants. So you are hostage."

Annie would have liked to know how, transported in the same little black car, she could be in the hands of the government one moment and the next in the hands of a gang with a grievance against the government. She could not believe that it was Small-and-Spritely's doing. It must be the driver, who was probably in league with the gang, or the boyos, who wanted a cut of the ransom money.

Gopala could explain. She could see him nodding at each stage in her predicament, frowning in pursuit of wisdom, then the click. Social welfare. The Indian way!

"How much do you want?"

"We demand the release of our brothers," the voice said. "We are not terrorists. We are fighters for justice and freedom."

"Yes, but you have an amount in mind for my release?"

"We are not mercenaries."

"Yeah, well, some fellow came in before you and said 'money, money'." She tried to sound impartial while informative, but what really bothered her was the lack of a game plan. She was in the hands of amateurs. She heard a sharp intake of breath. The cowled figure rose quickly and swept out, half-closing the bedraggled door. Raised voices were followed by grunts and dull thumps of body blows and cries of pain. Then silence.

The door scraped open again and the cowled figure returned. It was light outside and her eyes were becoming used to the dark. The cowl was a folded hessian bag, with slits at the armpits. The face was concealed by inclining the head. The figure moved swiftly across the room and crouched beside her.

"We are not mercenaries," the voice said. "We demand the release of our brothers."

"OK," said Annie.

"Government of India thinks that by putting them in gaol they are criminals. They are not criminals. They are freedom fighters."

"OK."

"Like Gandhi and Nehru. The British thought they could make them criminals by putting them in gaol, but look what happened. From the gaol they won freedom for the nation." He was enthusiastic about this point and wanted it emphasised. "From the gaol, the struggle was conducted for national independence!"

He had a way of making sense of what he was saying. Give him a podium, Annie thought, and he would weave a story in the air that would make an audience happy. He had none of the scholars' grievances, none of Gopala's moods, none of Ganguly's flights of fancy. She wished she could see his face.

"Well," said Annie, "why don't you let the brothers run your show from gaol?"

The shrouded figure was silent for a long time, not, she imagined, because he was considering carefully what she had said, but because he was upset by its implications. She could sense the tension in his body, the slow discovery of the fatal flaw in his argument.

"It is not yet the moment for a national uprising," he said soberly, then raised a clenched fist above his head. "Freedom for our brothers!"

"Alright," said Annie. "It was just a suggestion." Probably, in his imagination, he was the only one who could run the show from gaol.

He extracted from somewhere a piece of paper, which he thrust into her hand.

"Please read carefully. These are our just and proper demands. I will leave open the door so there is light to surmise the contents. I will return before several minutes have elapsed."

He departed, gently half-closing the collapsing door behind him. She turned the paper to the light and read:

Our Demands

1. Release of all those in prison, including Arjunan, wrongfully incarcerated on charges of sandalwood smuggling.

2. Compensation of fourteen crores paid by President of India to be distributed by Arjunan's personal hand among families of those wrongfully incarcerated.

3. Granting of 100-year licence to operate bauxite quarry in Madheswaran range in Mysore, the aforesaid licence to include authority to export.

4. Licences for two double-barrel (12 bore) guns, two pistols and two muzzle-loading rifles, necessary for protection of those licensed to operate aforementioned quarry.

5. Permission to create environmental farms around temples in forests, one in Tamil Nadu and other in Karnataka.

6. Approval to enter into negotiations for production of film based on life of Arjunan, to be shot in all languages officially recognised by Government of India and released nationwide at subsidised prices.

Annie's heart sank as she read down the list. Each item confirmed her fears; she was in the hands of a religious-cum-environmentalist cult or some local group with obscure grievances that would never be met.

She held out the piece of paper listlessly when the cowled figure returned.

"We wished you to know of our demands. We are not mercenaries."

"Well, not in so many words."

He responded by checking the document aloud, ticking off each item with a grunt and a cowl nod of approval.

"There's this quarry," Annie interrupted. "And compensation. Fourteen crores. How much is that?"

"It has been carefully calculated. Families have been deprived of income."

"And this film. Approval to ... whatever. What's all that about?"

"Film will carry message of hope to millions of Indians who are suffering."

"Well, maybe," said Annie. "It will depend on what kind of film it is, won't it? If it's just propaganda for ... well, you tell me."

"Film will be black and white. No singing and dancing. It will show value of self-reliance. It will show salvation of India by releasing energy and creativity of people, not by obeying laws of caste and privilege. It is very serious film."

"I'm sure it is." She hoped faintly that something might come of the conversation. "Arjunan is a friend of yours?"

"Arjunan is friend of all Indian people."

"He must be a very important person."

"Arjunan is humble servant of wisdom."

She would be taken to a temple in a forest and never heard of again. Except by the cult, who would turn her into a goddess. Esmiss Esmoor! Esmiss Esmoor!

"It's all very precise and particular," she said reasonably, "but there's nothing about a ransom. Where do I come in?"

The shrouded figure was silent. He went to the dissembling door and read again the piece of paper in his hand.

"Now you are here, that can be rectified." He straightened up. "A codicil will need to be issued."

"Like what? Give in to our demands or we'll kill her?"

"We will not kill you. We want Government of India to pay attention to our demands. That is our position. We are fighting for rights."

He slapped the piece of paper with the back of his hand to show his determination.

Annie gave up. She had more urgent needs.

"I need to go to the toilet. And I would love a cigarette."

"I will send someone," said the cowled figure. He touched her with his plump hand. "We will not harm you."

He turned at the door, flipping the piece of paper with the back of his hand in a businesslike manner.

"Is the spelling correct?"

"Yes," said Annie, in wonderment.

She was dozing in the gathering heat and wondering if anyone would come to take her to a toilet, or whatever was available, when shots rang out. She stared into the darkness, closing her eyes to try to imagine what was happening. The gunfire became intense. She could actually hear bullets striking the house, crunching as they sank in, whining as they ricocheted away. Then there was silence, followed by muffled voices that seemed to be shouting at each other across great distances.

The door creaked open and a cowled figure entered. It was a different shape from her earlier visitors. Its movements were swift and sinuous, even familiar. She could smell him as he crouched beside her. The cowl slipped back from his face and she could see the whites of his eyes. Even before he spoke, she knew who it was.

"You!"

Instant Gopala! She could not believe it. She wanted to scream with relief, hug him, smother him with kisses. Wheels within wheels. The Indian way! Click! But she was chained to the ridiculous pole and Gopala was, in any case, reproving.

"Shh. It is not wise to shout."

"Wise!"

She was brimming with questions tumbling over each other. But first she wanted to hug him to death!

"How did you get here? What's going on, for God's sake? Why am I here? Who are these people?"

A light smile played across his face. "Silly fellows."

"You can say that again," said Annie.

Her energy was returning and with it her jokey manner. If she had not been chained to a pole, she might have poked him in the ribs. But Gopala was examining her seriously.

"I will explain later," he said. "Just listen to me carefully. We are surrounded. There will be trouble any minute."

"What was that we just had?"

He searched her face for recognition of his seriousness.

"Real trouble."

He was a man of action, not weighing the consequences, intended and unintended, not contemplating imponderables, like history and destiny, just a person in a drama, looking for a straight line from point A to point B.

"You and I will escape out the back. Follow me. Don't ask questions. Just stay behind me, and everything will be alright."

Annie closed her eyes. She did not know what to say, yet she had to say something, something that would reach him, in the darkness, across the trouble she was in and whatever was going on outside the dilapidated house, across the cultural divide of their two countries, above and beyond the destiny of India and even the future of the world. Something that was as clear and direct as what he was doing. Something that was real, and would last forever.

"I love you, Gopala," she said.

He was about to release her as she spoke. His hands stopped on the chain around her waist. She saw him listen to her words in his head. His eyelids drooped modestly for a moment, then he wiggled his head and smiled his sad, brilliant smile. Her simple words, extruded under pressure, jolting in their unexpectedness, beautiful in their hallowed phrasing, uncertain in their implication yet clear in their intention, were received, absorbed and elegantly acknowledged. Click!

Then his hands unravelled the chain. She realised that the end without the padlock had been free. The Indian way.

He took one of her hands, eased her unsteadily to her feet, ran his strong fingers over her legs to massage her circulation. She was reminded of something. "I have to go to the toilet." He stood up straight, looked around the room, guided her into a corner's deeper darkness, turned his back politely. He raised a blind, opened a low window in preparation for their exit. When he felt her near him again, he squeezed himself over the sill, then reached back to help, lifting her through. Their eyes met. They smiled at each other with relief and pleasure.

"Just stay with me," he said.

She nodded, and ran, crouching behind him, away from the building into blinding sunlight. The guns were firing again. She heard the bullets striking the dilapidated house, crunching and whining. They crouched together by a water tank. He took her hand. Their bodies were so close she could feel his heart beating.

His eyes were razor-sharp, his hair bounced when he moved, his rubbery limbs were as taut as a tripod.

"Come," he said. He released her hand, stood. He pointed to some bushes on the other side of a dusty track, braced his shoulders for a quick dash like a runner at a standing start, and ran, the cowl bouncing at his neck. Should she run now, or wait until he was there, crouching beside the bushes on the other side of the track, waving her over?

Then she saw him fall. He fell in a canopy of grey dust. He did not move as the dust cleared in a slow swirl in the windless air.

She ran across the track, threw herself on the ground beside him. She put a hand on his leg, which was twitching, clutched his shoulders. His head was twisted and there was blood everywhere. She grabbed a hand, pulling it to her lips.

She was surrounded by men in uniform, who jerked her to her feet. She stared fiercely at Gopala's back. One of the men turned over the body with his boot. Annie shrieked at the sight of the bloodied face and tried to free herself, lashing out, but two men placed their hands expertly under her elbows and dragged her rigid body away.

In the cool, smoothly running, white police car, wrapped in the tweed coat, she kept her eyes closed. There was no conversation. She did not know where they were, where they were going, how long the journey would be. She did not care. All she could see was Gopala's body lying in the dust, a flickering image that never left the screen. They told her when they bundled her into the car that he was dead.

By the time they reached the small hotel, the image had become stable – the last shot in the film, establishing the mood and style, even the message, of all that had gone before, the camera's final tracking before the credits rolled.

That shot of Gopala's body meant that their affair was a tragedy.

It was the first time tragedy had entered her life. It was comedy before, even when painful. You smashed a plate or two, squeezed out a laugh and got on with it. What did tragedy mean, rhetoric more towering than life, ego more sublime, tenderness more intense? In real life, did it mean that someone was to blame? Was it something she had done or not done? If she had not had to go to the toilet, would it have been different? Or was it Gopala's mistake, an error of judgment that brought it on himself, his involvement, whatever it was, with the crazy kidnappers? Or were they both to blame? Was their affair so inappropriate, so improper, that it had burst a seam holding together India's vital parts? Or was tragedy life's normal course, the screams and tears of its victims no more nor less than the everyday feelings of human beings in a world without care?

It was business as usual at the Trilby, which meant that it was like any other middle-of-the-day. The bougainvillea was beginning to droop. The sweepers dusted the gravel drive in slow motion. Anyone who could legitimately escape the pale blue sky and the grey landscape was indoors. Two of the generals, busy at the reception desk, smiled and bowed as Annie approached, as if she might have been out sightseeing.

She did not conceal her contempt for them, now smiling and bowing as if nothing had happened, then scared and impotent as the boyos did want they wanted. It was impossible to convey to them what she had been through since she was bundled out in the middle of the night, but she would not let them think that the forces they were in league with had crushed and humiliated her. She had once regarded them as comrades. Now she did not hide the distaste in her voice. Everything she did from now on would be revenge for Gopala's death.

"You will need to renew the lock on the door of my room," she announced, bitterly calm.

"It has been done."

Of course. That was what the system was equipped to do. She waved a hand, mocking the marvellous simplicity of civilisation as practised at the small hotel. One of the generals handed her a new key, which she accepted without a word of thanks.

Her bed was made, with the fluffy quilt neatly folded. The room had been tidied, the bathroom cleaned. How long had she been away? It seemed like weeks, months, forever. She glanced at her watch: it was not yet 2.14 pm, twelve hours since she woke in fright. She discarded the boots and the tweed coat and flopped on the bed, pulling the quilt over her head and closing her eyes tight, slithering and squirming until she felt safe. Then, when her breathing had returned to normal and her head had cleared, she could feel strength returning to her limbs. She decided to shower, throwing off the quilt with sudden determination, jumping off the bed as if she had remembered an important appointment.

Under the shower, she washed her hair and then dried it with the blower provided. Standing in front of the bathroom mirror, she plied her body with lotion, lingering on soft muscles, dry patches and rounded corners. She put on her pale blue pyjamas, with the pink bear on the pocket encircled by throbbing hearts embossed in gold, brushed her hair up and down, backward, sideways, cleansed her face with cream. Attention to small things helped her to be calm. She slipped between the sheets and fell asleep almost immediately, but woke in an hour.

She sat in the rocking chair, looking at the old tree, thinking, thinking. The cat came and she touched it. It went and she forgot about it. Thinking, thinking. The sun left the window. She stayed, staring into the garden. Thinking, thinking.

Questions without answers, but her anger was real. Her anger with the men with guns who had killed Gopala was overwhelming. He was unarmed, running away from them. What right did they have to shoot him down? What right did they have to turn over his body with a boot, like a dog in the dirt? What right did they have to hustle her away, refusing to allow her to stay with him, refusing to listen to her explanation that he was helping her to escape? They controlled everything, the guns, the evidence, the law. Everything. She hated them. That was real.

Except that there was something else. What did she mean when she said "I love you, Gopala"?

Her life until now had been simple, a series of jolts, sometimes painful but always in the same direction, forward. It now seemed to have come to a stop. She struggled to find a meaning in what had happened, so that she could pick up her life again and give it direction. For those like herself who did not believe in life after death, the answer to death could not be life, which was itself doomed by nature. The answer to death had to be something that was part of life but not dependent on it to survive. The creations of art and the discoveries of science brought immortality to a few. For ordinary people death was held at bay by jobs and families, buying and selling, politics and sport, but they knew (because she had known) that these were not enough to keep the human story at the level they wanted, even when lifted and leavened with hope and ambition, desire and fulfilment.

Was love the secular miracle that gave life meaning?

She had never said "I love you" before, only read the words in novels and magazines, watched and heard them in films and on television, and wondered. At a university booze party, people lurched about singing "Drunk enough to say I love you!" Her family and boyfriends had not bothered with endearments. The words were themselves a surprise; they just came to her, as if she had been storing them up all her life, waiting for the right moment. She was sure this was the right moment. They were not tumbling on the big teak bed. He was trying to save her.

And now she had said them, they could never be recovered, tempered, explained, because he had heard the words and acknowledged them and was dead. If he were not dead, if he were alive, as was her expectation when the words had suddenly risen in her demanding to be said, what might she have said or done, or not said or done, so that the words could be fitted into their life together? But he was dead and she had to live with the words he had heard and acknowledged.

A melancholy anguish descended on Annie as she prepared to leave India. It was different from the tenderness that swelled in her throat whenever she thought of Gopala, different also from the waves of sadness after lovemaking. It was everywhere, yet nowhere in particular, like dusk creeping over the landscape. She had never felt this way before. She had always scrambled quickly out of depression, roused herself, pulled herself together. Sadness was unhealthy, a sign of weakness. It stopped you from performing at your best. You had to shrug it off.

This sadness would not be shrugged off. It was like the flu, insinuating its lethargy into her bones, insisting that she accommodate it, live with it, sleep with it. But she could not sleep. Strange obsessions kept her awake. What evolutionary blip, or sudden leap in cultural history, had brought some animals within range of human affection, so that they were loved, not eaten? Why had the flesh of cattle, sheep, pigs and poultry become acceptable on the tables of the Western world, while that of horses, dogs and cats had not? She peered into the eyes of the cat on the window. Pleased with her attention, it peered back with its light, golden eyes, sidled up to her, mewed affectionately, offered a paw. Cats were fickle, and she did not know whether or not she liked them, but the thought of eating them was repulsive. Could she drown them at birth, as her father had, in the local creek in a bag weighted with bricks?

Well? It wasn't enough to ask the question and leave the issue dangling in the air. Answer it! And don't say only if my father made me do it. It's not the same as asking the vet to "put down" your beloved best friend suffering from seizures in ancient age. Kittens are at the beginning of life. And don't say it's better for society to drown them than to let them loose to become feral. Face up to the moral question. Could she, of her own free will, drown them? No, she couldn't.

She scrolled her memory. There must be a reason for the fetishes of civilisations. Why was the cow sacred to Hindus and the pig unpalatable to Muslims? If Japanese thought the meat of whales was delicious, why were not Africans addicted to the flesh of elephants? Whales were more difficult to catch than elephants.

She buried her head in her pillow, but Iris kept appearing, not just to survey the coat and the boots with raised eyebrows, but protesting at the ungainly prospect of Indian prosperity. They are together on MG road, in a shopping mall in the New Delhi outer suburb of Gurgaon, a burgeoning call centre. No lolling Ganesh, no calcined temple, no intricate pediment of entwined human and animal forms, no fetid water tank. Instead, a pristine edifice, domed and colonnaded, with undercover parking, escalators and cheerful music. They brace together, ascending to consumer heaven, arms linked around their waists, looking out over the vast plain of modern India, fast food stalls, cinema foyers, automatic teller machines, supermarket checkouts, pharmacies. On their right are swanky clothes shops, the brand names of the Western world. On their left are the global latest in computer technology, television sets, video games and sound equipment. Behind are spacious showrooms of the furniture admired by India's aspiring middle class, designed to fit into the grand apartment blocks and the gated and lawned bungalow communities under construction down the road.

"It makes you think, doesn't it?"

What, indeed, could be done with all the junk if every Indian – and every Chinese – owned (Iris knits her thumb and forefinger, thrusting three fingers at Annie) a house, a car and a fridge, like the good folks of Gardenvale, and were cajoled into upgrading or renewing them by call centres, shopping malls, credit companies, governments and incessant advertising (five fingers in her face), so that jobs were created and the economy kept ticking over? And what indeed would the future be like if Christian fundamentalists and Muslim extremists had their way and global population exploded rather than declining in response to prosperity, as they were supposed to do? If there were more and more people wanting more and more things, would not planet earth shrug them off, in some cataclysmic fashion, just to survive? Was it the case, as Iris kept saying, that there were more people currently alive than had ever died?

"Where is India's celebrated poverty?" Iris asks, presenting the scene below with an elegant, disdainful hand. "You might ask whether there are beggars in India because poverty is widespread or because almsgiving is spiritually desirable."

You might indeed, and what answer might you get, the new tragic Annie asks herself, threshing the bedclothes. Exhausted with questions she could not answer, she needed something ordinary and human. She didn't even have a photograph of Gopala. She had nothing from the bungalow (like the creaking fan) to remind her of him, except a few scraps of paper with poems scribbled in Hindi on them that she had picked up from the floor and couldn't read. She had nothing from the residence. Or Mussoorie. Or the dilapidated house. Or the small hotel. All she had to take home from her visit to India, apart from a heavily-stitched, red canvas shoulder bag from the conference at the National Museum, was the 18th century temple piece she had bought at the beginning. And the coat and the boots. She had no presents for anyone.

She remembered the woman guard at Mrs Mehta's gaol, rang her mobile and arranged to see her. They met in a tea-room that was like an oasis of calm in the heat and fumes of Connaught Circus. Voices murmured over the soft clicking of cups on saucers. The warm, wet smell of aromatic leaves from Darjeeling, Nilgiri, Sikkim and Assam wafted past. They sat at a small, round, glass-topped table with mutual sighs of relief and pleasure. Not knowing why they were there, the woman was reserved, assuming that the meeting had something to do with Mrs Mehta.

"A gentle creature. Very English, poor thing." Anticipating probing questions, she gave an account of improving prison conditions. "A mobile petition box does the rounds so people can make their complaints without anyone knowing, like a secret ballot. And there's vocational training, around the clock medical services, including naturopathic and Ayurvedic. There's weekly poetry lessons. And organised sport, of course. We had a Say No to Drugs concert the other night as part of what they call ethical therapy. And there's a Quit Smoking program. The trouble is crowding. The gaol was built for two thousand and we've got ten thousand."

She made everything seem manageable in desperate circumstances and Annie nodded in sympathy. She did not care what they talked about. All she needed was the woman's reassuring presence.

"I'm going home and I just wanted to say goodbye."

"Oh, that's nice," said the woman.

She was wearing a simple cotton frock; her plump arms were enticingly bare. A swinging skirt reached just below her knees and her slim legs ended in sandals. She could have walked in from a stroll on an Australian beach.

"You don't wear the sari?"

"Weddings and funerals."

"It's so … enhancing. I thought every Indian woman would rely on it."

"My work gives me a jaundiced view of Indian culture," the woman said.

"When we met at the gaol, you were quite frank," said Annie. Even conversation about things that did not matter could be interesting. "About human rights."

"Did that puzzle you?" There was a twinkle in the woman's appraisal of Annie, as if she had encountered this problem before.

"Well, in Australia human rights are robust, like weeds. They don't need to be nurtured. People just assert themselves, not because they know they have the right but because it's their nature. It must be different in India?"

The woman had a habit of smiling while sitting back to absorb what you were saying. Annie waited. The woman was comfortable with what she knew, like the Man from Bangalore, and would explain herself eventually.

"You haven't noticed? We're all individuals in India." She surveyed the tea-room, customers absorbed in low conversation and the demure clicking of cups. "We're even more eccentric than the English."

A young man with a bright waistband and a tray held high flitted by, then twirled and swooped on their table, brandishing a jug of hot water.

"He thinks he's a messenger of the gods," said the woman guard, not bothering to lower her voice. "In his head are order, beauty and happiness. Outside is disorder, ugliness and misery, but he doesn't notice."

"And poverty?" said Annie, her rising Australian voice seeming to question.

"Oh, poverty," said the woman guard helplessly. "We're probably even poorer than the Chinese. I don't know the data. But the Chinese are practical, cheerful people. They're all little capitalists now, just as they were once all little communists. The herd moves as one and they are happy. In India, we are divided by religion, class which we call caste, and just about every fad and fashion you can think of. We are the greatest complainers in the world. Any slight is an injustice." She sounded like Pat, except that she enjoyed it. "Every Indian is embarked on a personal journey of self-improvement. Every community, every region in India wants to go its own way. We have militant vegetarians protesting about meat and fish in supermarkets! We are never happy. But worthy, in our own way."

She smiled at the predicament she and India were in. "I try to keep my mind on other things, keep myself busy."

"Reincarnation?" Annie ventured. "That puts a damper on ... things?"

The woman guard laughed reincarnation off the table. "It's in our bones. Believers and non-believers the same. Fate and destiny."

She smiled at Annie as if that might be enough for one day.

"If I were an Indian, I'd probably be in one of those non-government organisations fighting for something," said Annie, reluctant to release the woman. "Archaeology would seem like a pastime for idle hands."

"I love Spanish architecture," the woman said, then quickly explained herself. "Sorry, the connection is the arch." She continued cheerfully. "Spanish houses sit solidly on the ground, thick plaster walls, low-pitched, tiled rooves, courtyards and porches and balconies that seem to be part of the house, inviting you in, not just stuck on. Indian houses are either stone monoliths, forbidding you to enter, or wooden structures that are so flimsy they seem open to anything." She concentrated on a thought. Her good-looking, open face and short hair gave her a girlish look, making the effort seem earnest. "I must have a yearning for domesticity. When I see a Spanish house, I think of sanctuary. They are built to last and the people inside must be civilised. They will ask you in."

"You have a family?"

"I do." The woman shifted her eyes. "Two kids."

"And someone?" Annie was not certain of matrimonial niceties in India.

"Not now," the woman said. "That's why I'm in prison!" She laughed away the deliberately false phrasing. "I'm a single mum, which in India is no joke." She examined Annie, as if she might know the feeling, and then pulled herself together: "As I said, fate and destiny." She squared her shoulders and stared back at Annie, as if demanding to know what was next.

Annie took the hint and asked the woman where she shopped for clothes. "Not around here," the woman said, screwing up her nose. Far? Not really. Within minutes, Annie had paid for the tea, hailed a taxi and they were on their way to a market where contemporary Indian fabrics and designs were available. Everything was right, the material, the style, the price. Even the colours were right, not the etiolated mushrooms and taupes that were popular in the international boutiques, but soft, warm pastels that Annie associated with childhood. One thing led to another. Annie bought shirts and blouses for family, friends and herself, embroidered handkerchiefs and silk scarves for colleagues. The woman guard paraded and fingered each purchase, as if it were hers.

Annie piled her purchases into a taxi and they faced each other on a busy pavement. The woman lived nearby and would walk. She stood back, observing another foreigner leaving India.

"I'm so grateful. I knew I'd forgotten to do something, but it hadn't occurred to me that it was shopping." Annie was uncertain whether to kiss the woman, hug her, give her the namaste salute or shake her hand. "I never knew that shopping could be so guilt free," she blurted, wondering what she meant. She sensed they were pleased to have been together; they shared something, but it could not be explained, only experienced. While she was thinking how to bid farewell, the woman stepped forward and Annie felt soft, warm hands closing on her own.

"There's always something to do," said the woman. "Keeps you going."

She squeezed Annie's hand and gently moved it back and forth, like a delicate handshake. Then she stepped back. "Off you go with your goodies," she said, waving Annie on her way.

She did not know the woman's full name. She did not know the names of the two children, their ages, genders, nor anything of the ex-spouse or partner. Like the Man from Bangalore, it did not seem to matter. Yet they were the most normal people she had met, more like her than anyone else in the India novel she found herself in.

But they did not know the answers to the questions that she knew she would continue to ask herself in Australia. What was Gopala doing in the dilapidated house and who was responsible for his death?

15

"WHAT AN AWFUL THING," SAID Iris, on the telephone. "These gangs are springing up everywhere."

"Yes," said Annie.

"Taking hostages and that sort of thing. Just to embarrass the government or make quick money. Or both."

"Yes," mumbled Annie.

"You used to know what was what but now you can never be sure of anything," said Iris. "People you think are nice and sensible turn out to be crooks or fanatics, or both."

"Yes."

"You've had a dreadful time, Annie dear. You're welcome at the residence, of course."

"I'm alright. Thank you."

"Can I make a suggestion? Just a little one."

"Yes."

"Don't get involved," said Iris. "You never know where it will finish up."

"Yes," said Annie.

"Pat would like to see you," Iris said.

Yes, and she would like to see Pat. She needed to untangle the skein of conjecture and deception that clogged her thinking whenever she tried to understand what had happened to her. She felt like a minor character in a novel. All the other characters were larger than life, the events beyond her control, the plot so complex she couldn't follow it, the narrative written by someone who did not like her, even care about her. The ending was, literally, a dead-end. She needed to recover her professional competence, and a sensible conversation with someone who had made a profession of separating tactics from strategy might help.

They met for drinks in the big hotel near the Australian compound. A tourist promotion was underway. An elephant with sparklers in its ears and a phosphorescent trunk, surrounded by cameramen and their equipment, blocked the entrance. They walked around the back, by the swimming pool. Annie had once thought she and Gopala might swim together in this pool, as a kind of social coming out.

They sat near the pool in deckchairs dried pale by the sun. After a cursory inquiry, Pat ordered gin and tonic for two; it was the kind of drink you had when you did not care what kind of drink you had. Beer was clumsy and exotic drinks were celebratory.

Pat set out to be conciliatory. "I won't say I'm surprised, but you've had a rough time just the same, and I'm sorry."

"You're not surprised at what?"

"Well, you know my opinion of him."

He would prefer to leave it at that. It was hard for a gentleman to put into words the evidence for an opinion that he knew she did not share. He had wanted this meeting with Annie to clear his conscience about sacking Gopala. He wanted to demolish any connection in her mind between the sacking and Gopala's death. So far, the media had not made any connection. The raid on the dilapidated house had been treated as another crackdown on another gang, resulting in several arrests, "one fatality" and the rescue "without incident" of the (unidentified) hostage. The Australian high commission had not been mentioned. The only question was whether the gang was local or linked to an Islamist, Maoist or radical agrarian group. Gopala's name had been made public, but not his job at the compound. Pat wanted to keep it that way until Annie was safely out of the country.

Annie hoped that Pat would throw some light on why Gopala was there, in the dilapidated house. He would have been briefed by Gleeson, who would have been briefed by the police. Gleeson was insufferable and malicious, but he would have as good an account as anyone of the official version, including whatever had been picked up on mobile phones, dropped from eaves and recorded in innumerable interviews, like hers.

"He had a chip on his shoulder," said Pat. "A large one. The way he behaved with you was just an indication. I tried to warn you off, but that's water under the bridge."

"He was trying to save me." Annie glared at Pat over their glasses of gin and tonic. This was something she knew, only she knew, and it was her duty to make sure everyone else knew it.

Pat could not bring himself to think that she was actually grieving for Gopala, just as he did not like to think that his decision to sack Gopala might be linked with his death. He stayed with the big picture. The emotions of dispossessed and revengeful people were for tacticians, not strategists. How Gopala might be connected with low caste people trying to hold the government to ransom over piddling local issues was for others to work out. Also, the eurhythmics group. Ganguly and that woman Mehta were obviously an item. The hotel was some kind of safe house.

What happened was a symptom of something larger happening in the political culture of India.

"When governments make extravagant claims and promises, people like your man and that crackpot Ganguly come out of the woodwork with fancy ideas. Mix them up and law and order breaks down. Not because the army and the police don't know how to do their job but because they get caught up in the madness themselves."

"The little puffs?"

"Eh?"

Pat went on to explain that India was fortunate strategically. The Himalayas were a shield to the north and east and the sea surrounded the peninsula to the west and south, so it had only Pakistan to worry about. But tactically, you needed a firm hand internally to hold it together and with the end of the Cold War and the spread of globalisation, with religion and ethnicity on the increase, the caste system up for grabs because of election promises, and now terrorism …

"The centre is not holding," he concluded gloomily.

"You mean the police are corrupt?"

He was not prepared to go that far. The police were more subject to politics than the army, but both were basically professional. No, it was more that ... He waved his hands to suggest an imbroglio.

"Once the lid's off, the whole show tumbles out. No hierarchy. Anything goes." His laugh was empty. "It's getting like America." He mused. "Indian students in Australia complain about everything, when all they want is to live there." He straightened his shoulders. "Makes life difficult. Youth and energy are fine in their place, but they need direction."

He noticed her lower lip and tried humour. "I think I'll apply for Beijing. Respect for age."

She needed to pin Pat down. He could lay it all out for her, information graded according to source and reliability, tactics and strategy separated, the national perspective, stability and security, kept in sight, the international implications, balance of power, sub-regionally, regionally and globally, kept in mind. It would be as rational an answer as she was likely to get. But she knew it would not answer her question.

She explained carefully that she did not know how Gopala was involved with the gang, nor anything about Mrs Mehta, Professor Ganguly and the study group. She did not know how the same car and driver that took her for police questioning also took her to the dilapidated house. But she did know one thing. She was absolutely certain of one thing.

Pat waited for her to make the connection he did not want. She would remind him that he had promised Gopala would not be punished; he might miss out on promotion, but he would keep his job. He had broken his word. He would respond by reminding her that what he had said was based on the assumption she would remain at the residence, not disappear into thin air.

Annie spoke very slowly. "He-was-trying-to-save-me."

Pat listened courteously. "Yes." So Gleeson's briefing must have included the possibility, Annie thought. "Only after he got involved himself," Pat said.

Annie was determined. "Before he was killed, I told him something." She was steely. "I told him I loved him." She cleared her throat. "I used the actual words."

She waited, wondering how Pat would accommodate such raw intelligence. "I told him I loved him," she repeated, her eyes like laser beams. "I said the words. 'I love you, Gopala.'"

"Yes," Pat said.

"Now I've put you in the picture," said Annie, "I'd like you to do the same. What was he doing in the house? I know he was trying to save me. But why was he there in the first place?"

Pat knew the answer or thought he knew, which was all he could expect in such murky conditions. Gopala had decided on a payback for his sacking, which was to take Annie hostage, creating a media event that would expose their affair and embarrass Pat, the Australian high commission and the whole imperialist system of class, caste and skin colour. He had low-grade security connections through his job, but he bungled the exercise, crossing wires. The government got wind of it and primed for action in the emergency, swooped, only to discover she was in the hands of some kind of cult.

He took a deep breath and decided to say some of it. "We'll know more when we get the coroner's report, but there's a view gaining ground among police doing the investigation that your man arranged it himself."

Annie did not trust Pat. "You're joking."

"Well, you don't have to take my word for it. I'm just passing on, in confidence, what I've been told."

"You mean he kidnapped me!"

"He arranged it. He wanted a media event, but it all went wrong. My guess is that he arranged the whole thing to make a big fellow of himself by kidnapping you, and then some members of the gang decided to make some money out of it."

"But why should he want to kidnap me?"

Pat's open hands on the tabletop expressed his resignation.

Annie was silent. What had seemed ridiculous was now taking shape in her mind. She remembered old Vidya, the night she noticed that Gopala had become a man of action.

I am going today, dear friend,
And shall not fear the elders at home …
So much did I conceal

From fear of others,
Even the currents of my love.

"Why would he want to do that?" She was coping with the thought that it was the kind of thing that Gopala might do.

"Your guess is as good as mine," said Pat. He was relieved Annie did not seem to know he had sacked Gopala. If she did know she would have nailed him by now. He had thought she probably did know, and may even have been complicit in the hostage scheme. Now he knew it was better to leave that stone unturned. "Anyway, he was trying to save you," he said. "We know that."

Annie persisted with Pat because her failure to do so in the past had led her into trouble that might have been avoided, and he knew things she wanted to know, but she could not find the right approach. She had shown him her true colours over Gopala; they were doomed to differ on everything that mattered. Pat liked people who were successful, not just in a worldly, material way, but also in managing their feelings. Emotions that were out of control destroyed the distinction between strategy and tactics that for him was the difference between stability and turbulence, contentment and disquiet, even, perhaps, life and death.

It remained to rescue Gopala from Pat's disdain. "What about his poetry?" she asked, as if accusing him of something.

"Eh?"

"Have you read any of his poetry?"

"Not my cup of tea."

"Are you familiar with the work of Vidyapati?"

"Sorry," said Pat.

She recited:

"Radha, you are an ocean of nectar
And Krishna is afloat in it
Like a furious elephant."

Pat sniffed. "Sounds like India. Our cook's sweets are like spun sugar."

She decided to give it away. "I have to go now," she said, standing up.

"Do you have transport?" he asked. He did not ask where she was going.

"I'll get a taxi," she said grandly.

"Not at all." He offered her his car. She declined. He persisted. She refused.

They parted on the steps, he intending to walk to his office, she striking out in search of something with wheels that would take her back to the small hotel.

16

Mrs Mehta was released from gaol and was her old self, bearing ill will to no one.

"Things have slipped a bit here, but you were wonderful." She leaned across the table in her room with the three chairs, with a graceful toss of her sari over one shoulder. "We women have to stick together. Keep the home fires burning. Bring a bit of civility into the place." A pulsing lower lip implied she might not have banished entirely the memory of her troubles, but her eyes were alert again.

Her attitude to Gopala's death was a mixture of innocence and embarrassment. She fussed over the details, without shedding light on any of them. "It's not your fault, dear. He was a moody one. We should have realised he was over his head in something or other. But it's no use crying over spilt milk, is it? You'll be alright when you get back to your own country."

Her insouciance was supported by the public facts. The event that Annie thought had changed her life, that had sent tremors around the small hotel and the Australian compound, and had been recorded in the files of the police and government of India, received only minor public attention. The Indian media had bigger fish to fry than a scuffle with another sect with inscrutable demands or a brush with dacoits who had kidnapped a tourist. Gopala was not a celebrity. The great river of life flowed on.

Annie, however, was still under its spell.

"What do you mean, in over his head?"

"I had no idea what was going on, dear," said Mrs Mehta, obligingly. "And the professor was only involved because of me, poor thing. Such a warm-hearted man."

"How do you mean, because of you?" Annie tried to keep her voice down. She did not want to seem to be probing, even if she was.

"Well, you see, dear," said Mrs Mehta. "They were in this study group. They did yoga and things like that, but they were actually studying ..." She spread her hands and shook her head in testimony to her failure to understand what the study group was studying.

"They wanted to make the world a better place." She was sure of that.

"Have you any idea how I finished up driven in a police car to that place?"

"I've no idea, dear," said Mrs Mehta. Her eyes lit up suddenly with the wisdom of the ages. "Perhaps someone bribed the driver."

"What was Gopala doing there?" Trying not to sound inquisitorial, Annie sounded desperate.

"I'm very sure of that, dear. He was trying to save you. I'm sure of that."

Annie was grateful for Mrs Mehta's reassurance, but resisted her aura of certainty.

"Yes, but why was he there? He said they were his friends."

"I don't know, dear. But I'm sure he was trying to save you, very sure."

Professor J.P. Ganguly popped his head around the French doors, observed them silently, disappeared, and then returned, bowing himself in. Mrs Mehta excused herself and bustled off to the front counter.

"Before you say anything," said Annie, raising a hand in warning, "I want you to tell me why Gopala was there. In simple language that I can understand. I would also like you to tell me what you and Mrs Mehta and he were up to in the study group."

"Up to?" Professor Ganguly dutifully inquired.

"What was the purpose of this study group? Eurhythmics!" She waved and wriggled her arms.

"Study," said the professor.

"What?"

"The purpose of the study group was study," said the professor, stressing each syllable, like a lesson in piano scales.

"Oh, yes. Now pull this one." Annie offered a booted leg.

"Keeping our minds and bodies supple." Professor J.P. Ganguly gleamed and beamed, as if to demonstrate what a supple mind and body might be like. "Means to an end."

"So you don't know anything about someone called Arjunan and sandalwood smuggling, or a bauxite quarry somewhere or temples in forests or a film about this Arjunan to be shown at subsidised ticket prices so that everyone can see it."

Professor J.P. Ganguly listened carefully, shaking his head. "We are an undisciplined people," he announced. "There is too much freedom in India. Anarchy!"

Having explained the situation to his liking, Professor Ganguly crossed his ankles, waiting for her to stop waiting, beaming genially at her over his bow tie, tilting his head as if to entertain another perspective, perhaps of her, perhaps of something behind her. Her astral body? Annie closed her eyes in frustration.

"I have been examining new research on Gondwanaland," Professor J.P. Ganguly announced, as if to cheer her up.

"Before you go on," Annie interrupted sharply. "Just tell me this. Were you arrested, detained, apprehended, questioned? Anything?"

The professor's eyes opened in stages as she spoke, until they were wide with amazement, or dismay, she could not be sure, at the enormity of the question. After slowly subsiding, he extended one hand and slapped it lightly with the other.

"Animadversion," he said. Before she could ask, he moved on.

"The research is impressive. Gondwanaland is actually named after a region of Madhya Pradesh, inhabited at one time by the Gonds, an aboriginal tribe, but the research goes back as far as Sir Francis Bacon who noticed in 1620 how some of the continents fitted into each other. Then geologists and meteorologists became interested and lately palaeobotanists have taken it up. Not my field, but I can manage. They support the theory of continental drift on the basis of evidence of the distribution of flora – pecopteris, gigantopteris and glossopteris, for example. I am, of course, an ardent advocate of biomimicry. It explains the past very adequately and, if we practise it intelligently, will give us a sustainable future. It's the answer to global warming."

He observed Annie keenly, as if she might have been following what he was saying.

"The research suggests that India and Australia were once joined, together with Africa and Antarctica. It explains why your Aboriginal people are the same as ours, tall and spindly, not short and plump like the Melanesians and the Javanese."

Annie decided the only way to deal with the professor was to affect an icy coyness. "It was nice of you to drop in. Did you have something in mind?"

"I was just passing and thought it would be pleasant to renew our acquaintance. How is your project?"

"In abeyance at the moment. There've been a few interruptions, you might have noticed."

Her irony was translucent, but the professor had decided to leave. Indeed, he was halfway out.

"Mrs Mehta, for example." She had to shout quickly, to catch him.

"Yes, very unfortunate." But he was heading for the door. "An able woman." He was now at the door. "And warm-hearted." He turned for a last word.

"If it weren't for continental drift, we would belong to the same territory, share the same strategic imperatives." He raised a clenched fist in a gesture of camaraderie, holding his arm aloft and visible while the rest of him disappeared around the doorway. Professor J.P. Ganguly then disappeared completely.

17

ONCE MORE, SHE FACED MR Gleeson over his big, neat desk in his air-conditioned office. She had to sign a statement Pat had arranged for her to make so she could return to Australia before the coronial inquiry. She could have asked for the document to be sent to her at the hotel, but she had an ulterior motive. Gopala's family had handed over responsibility for his body to the compound. She could not bear having to ask the unconscionable Gleeson for a favour, but she wanted to see Gopala for the last time.

Mr Gleeson sat upright, regarding her with unconcealed pleasure. He rubbed his hands together. "Well, here we are again."

She explained her request, using plain words. "I would like to see the body."

"Yes, yes," said Mr Gleeson. "View the remains."

He sat with arms folded, observing her with a smiling face and eyes as flat and hard as stones. "For the last time." He might have been mouthing a prepared text were it not for the smirk on his lips and the malice in his eyes. "The remains are not here, you realise? Not here."

She nodded. She did not know where dead bodies were kept in India.

"Gopala Damodar has passed away, as they say." Mr Gleeson was playing out a long line, teasing his catch. "Or passed on." He wiggled his head to play with the distinction. "Actually, as you know, dead. Fatally shot."

He watched her carefully, as if he feared she might slip the hook. "A very mysterious business." He wrapped his mind tightly around the mystery. "A very mysterious business indeed."

"Solve it for me," said Annie sharply.

Mr Gleeson's smile was so small it did not leave his lips. "As you are aware, there will be a coronial inquiry, from which a finding on the cause of death will in due course emerge. In due course."

"Sure," said Annie, "but what do you think? Join the dots for me."

Mr Gleeson spread his upturned hands before her in a gesture that was, for him, almost intimate. "Who am I to have thoughts on such a delicate matter?"

She tried to calculate what was in her enemy's mind, but she knew he wanted to hurt and humiliate her, so she sat tight.

"You want to view the remains, Mrs, Miss, Ms ...?" It was hard to detect which title he disliked most.

"I would like to see the body." She nodded, giving grudging approval to the conversation so far.

Even dead, Gopala was more real to her than all the lively bodies swirling around her. She wanted to add something to the four last words he had heard, so that she could take them back with her to Australia, make them real, not leave them behind as part of the mystery and tragedy of India. She told none of this to the reprehensible Gleeson, who wriggled his plump body in his official chair behind his official desk and explained to her that under Indian law, empowered, as he was, to act for the family of the deceased, he was obliged to ask why someone without any legal right of access to the estate, which included, of course, the remains of the deceased ("mortal remains"), should seek the privilege of viewing the body of the deceased ("body of the deceased").

She did not answer.

"Is there a particular religious reason for the request?" Mr Gleeson's eyes glowed with satisfaction. "I take it you are not Hindu, Ms ...? Not Hindu."

"No," said Annie, looking him coldly in the eye.

"You do not wish to ... actually handle the body in any way? Handle the body. Bathing, oils, flowers, that kind of thing?"

Annie knew what he was doing. She knew he knew, and he knew she knew. In this enclosed world, they tested each other's strengths. Nothing would make her explain anything to him. She had never trusted him, and every moment with him assured her she was right.

"No."

"You just wish to view the body? To pay respect?"

Annie was now looking beyond Mr Gleeson, but she could imagine his twisted lips.

"Yes."

"You realise that you may be given an opportunity to do this at the cremation ceremony? You may be allowed to approach the bier. Approach the bier. Given permission to stand by the body before the fire is lit."

Mr Gleeson seemed far away, communing with this possibility. Then he answered himself. "I am forgetting. You will not be here. In any case, you would not wish to pay your respects in public. Not in public. You would wish to view the body in private. In private. As befitting a private relationship."

He had landed his catch and now held it in his hand. "A very private relationship."

"Yes," said Annie.

She steeled herself against turning her back on him and walking out. He could no longer hurt her. She had no need to hit back at him, placate him, manage him, do anything with him. He was just a door with a rusty hinge. He would open eventually. The silence continued. Their eyes met and she declined to acknowledge him in any way. He was nothing. Yet, of all the people she knew, he was the most likely to know why Gopala was in the dilapidated house.

"What was he doing there?"

"Ah," said Mr Gleeson.

It was his kind of question. You could have all the theories and opinions in the world, have influential social connections, have emotions as subtle and delicate as a flower or as powerful as a cruise missile; none of this was as valuable as a fact. Facts were information and information was his property. Information was what people wanted. His job was to see that only those who had the right to know were informed of the facts in his possession. She knew she did not qualify.

"A good question," said Mr Gleeson.

"Well, what's a good answer?" She disliked the bluster in her voice, but with Gleeson, it came naturally.

Speculation was not his strength, he explained, although he was quite capable of handling complex matters. "Complex matters." In a competent manner. "Competent manner."

"Speculation is one of humanity's natural advantages," said Annie airily. "You're human, aren't you?"

"Indubitably," said Mr Gleeson, containing himself. "I do not have to ask the same question of your good self."

She wondered, if she had been closer to Mr Gleeson, whether she would have slapped his face. She had never slapped the face of anyone, male or female, and realised quickly that it was something you did without thinking, or not at all.

She stood up instead. "Well, give it a go, try being human. What was he doing there?"

"Who knows," said Mr Gleeson quickly. "They didn't keep minutes of their meetings." His tone was resentful, and also respectful. Minutes of meetings contained information that had been tested and was reliable, real facts that he could possess and protect. "We have to wait for the court hearing. All will be revealed in good time."

"Very convenient," said supercilious Annie, rising on her heels.

Impervious to scorn, Mr Gleeson was prepared to elucidate, but not to a lady standing over him. "Please be seated." His tone was compliant and she complied.

"Very inconvenient, if I may say so, including for your good self. If our friends the police had not acted as they did, who knows what might have happened. Even to you, dear lady. Even to your good self. Sometimes our friends lose patience. Regrettably. But they had to act. And they did."

"Stop beating about the bush," Annie thrust at him. "Was this a set up? You and the police?"

"A set up?" He turned the phrase over, as if for the first time. "What an extraordinary idea, dear lady."

"Gleeson," Annie said. "Do one thing before I depart these shores. Give a straight answer to a question."

"Dear lady," said Mr Gleeson. "A straight answer requires a straight question."

"What was he doing there? That's straight enough."

"There is the big picture and the small picture," said Mr Gleeson, as if to a child. "No matter how closely I may wish to work with the Indian police on the big picture, we do not control the desires of the heart. Or, for that matter, the flesh."

She brushed his words aside, as if they were tendrils in her face. "He was trying to rescue me."

"That might seem, on a superficial reading of events, to be a plausible interpretation," said Mr Gleeson. His tone was heavy with reluctance. "The deceased was killed while trying to escape from the house. With you. With your good self. But your question was, if I remember correctly, something different."

He paused in his most portentous manner.

"What was he doing there? For an answer to that question we will have to wait for the coroner's finding. We will all have to assist the coroner, including the overworked person you see before you, to ensure that his finding is consistent with the facts, as they are known even now. Even now, dear lady."

"Well, give me a fact that is known even now," said Annie. She'd had enough experience of Gleeson to know that he was leading her somewhere.

Mr Gleeson examined his fingernails. He inquired of his guest if she would like a cup of tea, which she declined with an impatient flick of her head. He pursed his lips, drummed his fingers on his desk.

"A fact known then, but still not widely known, would be that the High Commissioner in his wisdom had terminated the employment of the deceased. Officially, this was for pilfering petrol but in the mind of the deceased, other factors may have been seen as relevant."

"Pat sacked Gopala?"

"You have expressed the fact in your inimitable way, dear lady."

"So ...?" Annie had a fleeting glimpse of Gopala, man of action.

"You asked me to connect the dots. It is for the coroner to do that. But it would seem within the realm of probability that the deceased was upset by the loss of his livelihood, at a time when jobs are scarce and jobs on secure and, if I may be allowed to say, high ground like the Australian high commission are a prize beyond accounting. Beyond accounting."

"So …?" So it was revenge and a ransom for lost earnings. Gopala was suddenly real.

"Who am I, dear lady, to pontificate on human weakness."

"Why not, you pontificate on everything else."

Mr Gleeson paled slightly, but remained in control of himself. It was his day, not hers.

She knew she would never learn from him all the facts, only those that served his purpose. He might or might not know why she was taken from her hotel by the police, or why she was taken to the dilapidated house, but he would never tell her. He might or might not know of a connection between the study group and the hostage gang, but he would never tell her. She was a pawn in a game, wheels-within-wheels, but in his eyes, like Pat's, she was not innocent. When she had backed Gopala in the petrol scam, she had taken sides, not only against him, the compound, the security of property and law and order. She had crossed the line between two community standards.

And she had done so because she could not resist the lure of the flesh. She had betrayed her culture for the primitive satisfaction of a powerful thrust from the loins. "Thrust from the loins." Gopala's. The despicable Gleeson was right. She had crossed the line.

On her way to the door, she knew she was glad she had defied him, the compound, her community, Western civilisation and anything else he might like to throw at her. She was glad she had ridden the high ridge between pleasure and pain. She was glad she had the strength to defy the Shards, to tell Small-and-Spritely everything, letting the facts fall where they may. He had probably read what she told Small-and-Spritely. That would have shaken him up!

Most of all, she was glad she had seized the moment in the dilapidated house to say those four words.

What she had meant, or what her words would have meant if they had escaped safely together, she could not say now, even to herself. But she had meant it when she said it. She saw him crouched at her feet, disentangling the chain, looking up, a man of action caught in the act, a moment of truth. Still life. She saw his face again, his sad, brilliant smile, acknowledging her message. He was trying to save her and now he was dead because of her. Everything else was speculation, legal nip and tuck, political buck passing and point scoring, non-minutes of meetings and minutes of non-meetings. Gleeson's world.

She was glad she was not of that world. She was profoundly satisfied that she had managed to say, "I love you, Gopala."

All this passed through her head as she paused at the doorway. Gleeson was still playing the game with her, but she had moved on. Big Game or little games, it made no difference. She had been foolish to try to make human communication with him. Now, all she wanted before leaving was to mark him with her disdain. She turned and faced him, a young Australian woman who had undergone a tragic experience in a foreign country and would not be denied her rights.

"I want to see the body," she said.

Mr Gleeson threw the fish back into the water. He had had his satisfaction. And perhaps she would go higher, forcing him to endure a lecture on non-discretionary consular duties and the rights of Australian citizens. You could never tell with diplomats. Consular officials knew what was what, and what wasn't worth bothering your head about. Diplomats were like politicians, always wanting to look good.

He transformed himself into an attentive consular official with duties to perform and explanations to give.

"I will make arrangements. He is nearby, in a manner of speaking. It was too far to send the body back to the family. Too costly. They are not, you might say, wealthy. Not wealthy." He primly pursed his lips, wiggled his head in the Indian manner and scribbled on a piece of paper. He held the piece of paper in his hand, without offering it. "For the last time," he said.

She walked quickly across the room and snatched the paper from him.

18

HOW BIG THE BODY WAS. It would be clothed in seamless white for the bier, but now his chest was bare. Two young men, who were doing something to the head, asked if it would be alright as it was, for her to see.

"Yes," she said.

They stood by, as if she might need assistance, but she motioned them away.

"I can manage," she said. She adopted the tone of finality she had learned at the residence, turning requests into orders. They filed out through a doorway, holding hands.

Dead Gopala dominated the room. Lying flat on a table, his body had spread, which is why it seemed so big. The coils of tension, the muscles, had subsided, the flesh looked heavy and smooth, like something washed up on a beach after a storm.

Annie stood by the body that had been her hard, black statue, her furious elephant, her sure-footed leopard, her horse, her little boy. She closed her eyes and touched a shoulder. It was cold.

Perhaps it would be different if she uncovered his head, she thought, but she did not wish to be reminded of the agony of his death. His head was bandaged, covering the wound. His forehead, his closed eyes, his nose, his lips, his cheeks, his chin were concentrated by the bandaging, so that they formed a physical grouping of their own, projected in a gruesome pout. She could hardly recognise him. It crossed her mind that she would like to see his body, but she was embarrassed by the lurking presence of strangers and too awkward in the presence of a dead body, even Gopala's, to unclothe it.

What she had wanted did not happen: the memories did not flood back. So she stood with her hand on his shoulder, forcing herself to be content with touching him. She tried to reach him with words. "You, you," she said, as she had said to the cat. She peered at his distorted face. She sounded as if she was disputing something, trying to convince him in some distant argument, or was annoyed with his body for being cold and unresponsive, or was complaining about the inconvenience of having had to come to see him. There was no affection in her voice, no intimation of loss or guilt, just an assertion, as if others might be listening.

She looked again at the body, hoping that she might find a clue in something remembered, like his smile, which she did now remember, so that the muscles of her face quivered.

If only there was a ritual she knew, even a small part of a ritual, that would give her the words or gestures she needed to express her feelings. A prayer, perhaps. She had no religious upbringing, no personal experience of death and she had not come prepared with meaningful words. She had seen on television women in foreign countries throw themselves weeping on the bodies of husbands and sons, but Gopala was neither and she was not going to throw herself on a dead body.

What was appropriate for whatever it was that Gopala had been to her? There must be something. But she could only glare thoughtlessly at his dead body. She saw it disappearing into flames. She saw mountains and crackling stars, the black void of the plains. The Five. She heard the whirr and the click, the wheels within wheels. Little puffs. The Indian way.

Then a line of poetry welled up from some childhood discovery of love and death that had seemed right at the time, a perfect ending, poignant.

"And you shall kiss me with a last kiss."

They had never kissed, just as they had never held hands. There was no need for sexual foreplay, nor social opportunities for displays of affection or tenderness. She wondered about the history of kissing in India. Old Vidya was brimming with erotic imagery but she could not recall an amorous meeting of lips. Gopala was against Bollywood. Did they kiss in the Mahabharata?

This last kiss would be their first, even more tangible than the four words she had impulsively uttered in the dilapidated house. She steadied herself, steeled herself, and approached Gopala's body. She leaned over and brushed her lips on the cold purse of his mouth, and then stood back quickly and shivered.

There was a commotion at the door as an elderly man in white dhoti, leaning on a walking stick, entered the room. He stood for a moment, waggling the stick in front of him, and then advanced towards her.

"I am the father."

Gopala would have been like him if he had lived long enough. The walking stick was deceptive; he needed it because he was almost blind but it was a weapon more than a crutch. He swung it before him as he walked. His limbs were full and firm and his hunched shoulders were heavy. His face, if moulded once by despair and suspicion, was now contorted with anger. He fixed her with a fierce stare.

Annie stood still and fearful as he approached, swinging the stick in front of him. He reached the other side of Gopala's body and his stick reached over it and touched her chest. He prodded soft flesh, and then, with a short, quick swing, he clouted her on the side of her head. She shrieked and stepped back. He touched Gopala's body, felt his way around it, and approached her again.

She was mesmerised by the old man. She stood still, waiting for him. His stick touched her, he prodded, measured the distance, swung. This time she raised her arm and warded off the blow. But he was relentless, his stick extended, wanting to touch her, his face grim and determined, his body balanced like a fighter's on the balls of his feet. She retreated, he followed. He stumbled against furniture, grasped it with his free hand, shoved it aside. She side-stepped and backed away but his stick followed her like a divining rod. He touched her, measured, swung. She parried, retreated.

Eventually, he cornered her. He prodded, measured, touched the wall each side of her with his stick and stood squarely in front of her, breathing heavily with satisfaction. She was powerless. His blindness, his physical strength, the walking stick wielded as a weapon, that he was the father, her knowledge of how his mind worked, and the conclusion they shared that

Gopala was dead because of her, these gave him authority over her. Unable to move, she awaited her fate.

Gopala's father was savouring, however, another stage in her punishment, which was the lash of his tongue.

"White slut! You killed my boy with your dirty ..." He pointed between his legs. "Foreign whore!"

"I am very sorry about Gopala," she said. "Truly sorry." Her drawing room phrases were toppled by his stare.

"Dirty ... twot," said Gopala's father.

She remembered the house in Gardenvale and the bundles of fireworks. It was all she could think to say. She said it.

"Sticks and stones
May break my bones,
But names will never
Hurt me."

Gopala's father listened carefully, an ear cocked. He turned her over in his mind, tasting before eating. For the first time since he had come into the room, he smiled. It was not a pleasant sight. It started with his lips and spread over his face, without touching his eyes. It ended in a widening of his lips in which there was no element of pleasure, no hint of humour. It was a smile of salacious satisfaction.

"You'll never get another one like that."

He licked his lips. She imagined him pouncing on the big teak bed. His harsh voice expressed his bitterness, his anger and his shame, but also his pleasure in doing what he was about to do to her.

"I banish you from India!"

"I'm going anyway," she said, holding some ground.

"You cannot live in India and you cannot live without India," he said, raising his free hand slowly as in benediction. "That is my curse."

He gestured at Gopala's body with his stick. "You will always want." His terrible smile distorted his features. "Never have."

They stood facing each other, an old man with piercing, sightless eyes and a pink-cheeked young woman whose darting eyes were lowered. Neither wished to make the first move. Saliva frothed at the corner of his lips and he flicked it away as he glared at her, his hand still raised, his stick clenched ready to swing, his legs braced. She cowered in the corner, her right hand against the wall, her left hand open to protect her face, her freckled nose catching bronze tints in her hair.

She was swamped with memories of Gopala. She could hear him laughing, see him tumbling on the big teak bed. He pirouetted, wiggled his coin-face, pursed his lips, bowed over his fingers. She saw him lying curled after lovemaking, black skin on white sheet on brown wood. The sweet flesh, the hard power, the high ridge.

"Falling in Love Again." Why had he liked that silly song? She could not fathom his taste in music. He loved "Smoke Gets in Your Eyes" and "Blue Moon". He would croon to himself in a style modelled on Dean Martin's, saying "noo", not "new". Then he would assert that Indian music was the best in the world, more beautiful in its controlled complexity than any other.

She broke down in front of the father, not caring any more about India's destiny, wheels within wheels, the click. Tears flooded her eyes, streamed down her cheeks. It would always be like that now, a piercing, heartbreaking tenderness. She no longer cared what Gopala was doing at the dilapidated shack, whether he was her captor or her rescuer. She no longer cared about an appropriate ritual for his dead body. The flames, the puffs, the Five. All over, Red Rover!

She had had enough of this old man with the walking stick. She lowered her arms and tensed the muscles in her legs, ready to spring as she watched Gopala's father come at her, eyes blazing, tongue out to catch the drips, stick ready to strike. She lifted one brown-booted leg and kicked him. She saw her heel hit him somewhere between chest and stomach and he crumpled and fell. She slipped past him without a thought, past, without a glance, Gopala's body lying on the table, through the door, past the two young men seated listlessly on a couch.

Out into the glare and clamour of the world.

19

ON THE WAY TO THE airport, Annie stopped the taxi when she saw the bookshop. They might have it. It was no use trying at the terminal. They would only have the same hefty paperbacks that sold at airports around the world. This would be a slim volume and only a real bookshop, like this one, would have it.

"Do you have the poetry of ... V-i-d-y-a-p-a-t-i?"

She was pleased that she got it right. She saw Gopala's bowed head, hands clasped and tilted in salute. The young woman behind the counter swivelled her eyes as she tested her memory. "I am new here." She took her apology a step further. "This is actually my first day."

"About Radha and Krishna." Annie's heart skipped a beat.

"Love songs?"

"Yes." The words echoed like a tolling bell.

Bind me in your arms, bruise me with your thighs ...
Lock me day and night in the prison of your heart ...
And:
The moon spits fire ...
Bird of spring,
Why do you torture?
Why do you sing ...?

The young woman led her through towering stacks at the back of the shop. "Yes, here we are," she said, extracting a slim volume from the shelves.

"The only copy." Annie took from her a pocket-size book containing one hundred "Love Songs" (in bold red) from a "Fourteenth Century Poet of Passion and Love" (in modest blue), entwined with line drawings of flowers and images of female eyes, lips and breasts.

Annie turned the pages, craving, dreading what she might find. She was on the high ridge again. Each toll of the bell tore at her heart.

"It looks interesting," said the young woman. "I'm sure I will read it, if we can get more copies. When I'm more experienced, I will find time to read on the job, without ignoring customers, of course."

Annie lived again the night in the garden. She walked backward from the big, luminous house, its cocktail cries ringing in her ears, into the damp, layered air of the pond. His voice came out of the darkness, his spirit became form, his form took shape. She could feel the dull glow of the garden pulling her down and she saw again the vast night soaring over them. Their shapes, their forms, their bodies, were irresistible to each other. She remembered so clearly that she cried out.

"Is everything all right, madam?"

Annie was surprised to be addressed as madam. She had packed the coat and the boots and was in casual wear for the long flight, grey slacks and cream shirt, low heels, the arms of a navy blue jumper tied around her waist. Perhaps Vidya's verses would seem silly to this admirable young person, who was far too sensible to be drawn into love and tragedy. But might not the same have been said about herself a few weeks ago?

"By the way," she said at the counter, as the girl took her money, "did Krishna actually exist?"

"Exist?" The girl was delighted to be able to answer such a simple question. "Of course." She elaborated. "The dark one. In Indian paintings, he is usually blue."

"Where did he live?"

"Live?" That wasn't the sort of information young women in bookshops were expected to carry in their heads. "Being a god, it is not easy to say where he actually lived. He pops up in lots of places." She smiled at Annie as if she might understand the wilful behaviour of gods. There was a reference book, however, through which her fingertips nimbly found a way. Her eyebrows rose and fell as she read. "Elder brother Balarama, a ploughman and heavy drinker, son Pradyumna and grandson Aniruddha … not much known." Her head began to wriggle. "Ah, yes. He lived in Mathura, which is near here. On the way to Agra."

"Really." Annie was surprised that the place was so real you could be directed to it. Krishna lived for her in "the light of setting suns, And the round ocean … and in the mind of man:" One man in particular.

"You can take a tour to visit the Taj Mahal, and stop in Mathura," said the young woman helpfully. She was again reading, a slender finger tracing a story. "Radha lived nearby …"

"Really." Annie had been so absorbed in the world of Gopala-Krishna that an independent existence for Radha had not registered.

"It doesn't say where," said the young woman. "Typical. They have where the man was, but not the woman." She shared the exasperation of sisterhood with Annie by lifting her eyebrows. Then, with a smile that invited confederacy, "She was a married woman, you know."

She swayed from the waist, like a dancer with ankle bells and tattooed feet. "Radha was flirtatious. You had to be to catch Krishna."

"Yes," said the new, tragic Annie. She had stopped Gopala in full flight on the subject of Krishna's domestic arrangements.

The young woman had discovered something she wanted to show Annie: an illustration of a painting of Krishna and Radha exchanging clothes. "If it weren't for his colour, it would be hard to know which was which." She was brimming with information. In old India, in the south, gods were male and female. She swayed her shoulders above locked fingers. It was sometimes hard to tell the difference. In Madurai, they worshipped a goddess. Here was Krishna picking flowers, playing the flute, dancing and flirting with the gopis. The young woman was right, he was ambidextrous, adored by the men, because he was irresistible to women, and by the women, because he was light, like them.

"We are lucky with our Indian gods. We don't have father figures up in the clouds. Our gods are down here with us, doing ordinary things." She mouthed the word. "Incarnate." Krishna was the eighth incarnation of Vishnu.

"Has there been a ninth?" asked open-minded Annie.

"Oh, yes." The young woman was enjoying her unexpected role as teacher. "Prince Gautama Siddhartha. He was the ninth." Her hands reclaimed and explored the reference book. "You call him the Buddha." Her slim finger nailed him. "He was born in what is now Nepal in 563 BC. When thirty years of age, he abandoned the court, his beautiful wife and all his earthly possessions."

She puzzled over a section on Hindu theology, then announced: "His mission was to end the ritual of sacrifice, to show compassion for animals."

"Did Krishna have a ... mission?"

Eyes bright, the girl recited from memory. "The deed itself, not the result." She struggled with the concept, returned to the reference book, creasing her forehead. "The ethical problem of action."

"I know about that," said Annie, remembering some bad advice in the Bhagavad Gita. "And a tenth?"

"Not yet. His name is Kalkin. He will take the form of a man on a white horse, with a flaming sword, who will judge the wicked of the world."

"I prefer Krishna and the cowgirls," said agnostic Annie, a secular humanist returning home after a dip into religious India.

"You could take a tour," suggested the young woman. "I'm sure it will be organised properly."

"It's too late, I'm afraid. I'm leaving. On my way to the airport."

"On your next visit, perhaps."

"I've been banished." Annie checked the young woman's anxious face. "Joking. I'm returning to my own country."

"I'm sure your country is as nice as India," said the poised young lady. She juggled a brown paper bag and a roll of sticky tape.

"Don't bother," said Annie. "I want to read it." She held the book of poems clasped to her breast. "I have had an experience in India."

The young woman had not expected such a personal revelation across the counter on her first day. Her eyes lowered, she returned the sticky tape to a drawer.

"A tragic experience." It was an unexpected phrase, more categorical than she intended, but the young woman showed sympathy with her gentle eyes, without going so far as to inquire what the tragic experience had been.

"But one that I do not in any sense regret." The gentle smile on the young woman's lips did not match her eyes, which had become watchful. Annie wondered if she could say, in a few words, how she would be different, now that tragedy had entered her life. Could she explain all that, with the taxi waiting?

She remembered the scribbled poems. She smiled warmly at the girl to allay any impression that she wished to seem mysterious.

"I am taking with me some original Indian poetry."

"Oh, that's nice." The charming girl was pleased, after preparing herself for something less innocent from this intriguing visitor.

"In Hindi," said Annie.

"Yes, of course."

"They will have to be translated."

"Of course." The girl's eyes were wide open, like the eyes of a child about to be told a story.

"When I come back, we can talk about finding a translator," Annie told the girl, as if they had already discussed the matter. She decided against leaving her name. The girl would not easily forget their encounter. She would make a point of coming to this bookshop on her return visit. They would order things for her and put them aside for her to collect. It would be her special place, like the small hotel and the library.

"Well, I'd better be getting along. Don't want to miss the plane."

"Writers are wonderful," said the young woman. "Don't you think? Brave, truthful and humble."

A gracious and discreet attendant had become, without warning, a pilgrim, intrepid and passionate. Annie felt the presence of India, the enigma of truth and hope in the midst of helplessness.

"The real ones, I mean. Not the show-offs." She waved hands. "That's why I work here. Surrounded by them. People say bookshops will disappear because of the Internet, but I don't care." She waved her hands again. "I love it here!" She paused, became thoughtful. "There's just one thing."

"Yes," said Annie, helpfully.

"When I come to the end of a book, I am so in need of a happy ending that I plead with the author." She raised her eyes to Annie, baring her soul. "You've taken all this trouble, and you've been so truthful and brave, can you not manage an ending that does not leave everything up in the air, asking me to work out what happens afterwards." She waited for Annie's reaction to her weakness. "I love happy endings."

Annie took the girl's hands, softly, as the woman guard had taken hers. "Have you a card?" she asked the girl. "In case I want to write ahead, order books – that sort of thing."

"Of course." The girl embraced the future, excited by what had happened on her first day. "I'll put my mobile number on the back, in case you want to ring outside office hours."

Annie departed in a flurry of promises and farewells. In the taxi, she opened the book. After a few pages, Vidyapati's sympathy with Radha became clear. For a 14th century poet, he was surprisingly sensitive to the intense and personal turmoil of a young woman who was entangled with a roving lover of unbounded lust and domain ("stubborn with experience" in one poem). She turned back to the book's introduction, which confirmed her intuition.

"Krishna is accepted for what he is – a delightful charmer, a marvellous lover. But he is ... regarded as callous, cruel, selfish, the very opposite of one who naturally inspires devotion, sympathy and appreciation. Radha, on the other hand, is Vidyapati's true heroine. Her ... slowly awakening youth, her physical charm, her shyness, doubts and hesitations, her naïve innocence, her need for love, her surrender to rapture, her utter anguish when neglected – all these are described from the woman's point of view and with matchless tenderness. Vidyapati, it is evident, loved and admired the female temperament and nature."

She turned the pages with renewed vigour, searching for evidence that that last kiss had not been an imposition. And she found it, in a poem that Gopala had recited on the big teak bed, but without these two lines, "With all her force/ She kisses her lover's lips" and (on page 42) "He drank my lips/ Pressing his face hard on mine" and (on page 88) "Have you then wiped away/ Our first kiss?" and (page 89) "And then with tender care/ Studies the love bites on her lower lip."

She wanted to laugh with relief, which she did. Gopala didn't really understand old Vidya. Or women. He probably didn't understand India either. He had his father's bleak view of everything to contend with, which admittedly was enough to send anyone off the rails. He just couldn't accept India as it really was.

Which was? She contemplated essential India, the form of India, Indianness, and her confidence collapsed. What did it mean to be an Indian? There was a god for every human attribute. Was Small-and-Spritely India, or the woman guard or the Man from Bangalore, or the president, who was recently an Untouchable, now a Muslim, or the prime minister, who was a Sikh, or the leader of the governing party, who was a woman born in Italy. Was India a multicultural society, like Australia wanted to be? She laughed at the thought.

Life, that huge, adulterated hash, that was India. Call it destiny or chance, history or culture, allegory or parable, give it form and shape, numbers and equations, inputs and outcomes, rewards and punishments; name it success and failure, it was always the same. No matter how deep you dug, it would always be there. Life with a capital L, where the dots are never connected. That was India.

She knew. She had been alive in it. She turned the page and read:

"On this earth
In wavering life
Youth is short-lived.
Enjoy it as you can
Or stab the heart.
O lovely girl,
Where is your wisdom?
The wealth of youth
Is yours
To be offered as a gift.
Give it as you will
It still remains.
Only he is poor
Whom you deny ..."

He was a wiz, old Vidya. You open the book, he has something to tell you.

As the taxi picked up speed on the airport road, Annie looked forward to going home. Compared with the civilisations of the world, Australia was second-rate, as many of its gifted sons and daughters proclaimed; not much to offer in the way of elevated thoughts, truth and beauty. Nothing metaphysical about Australia, very down-to-earth, a laboratory of the here-and-now. Well, there was something to be said for being ordinary. She laughed: Australians knew what was in the water. And it would be a relief to turn her mobile on again.

She would defy the curse of the father. She would not be banished. She would come back on her own terms. She was stronger now that tragedy had entered her life. She was not its victim; she had recovered from it a certainty that would be with her for the rest of her life. He had heard the four words and acknowledged them. The moment had become eternal. Because she had said "I love you, Gopala", death had lost its sting.

She turned and waved at the land she was leaving. As she waved, she clenched her fist to show her determination. Settling back in her seat, pleased with her salutation, she noticed the driver's eyes in the rear-vision mirror observing her calmly.

"Indiuh!" he said, chuckling and wagging his head.

"I have had an experience here," said Annie. Esmiss Esmoor! Esmiss Esmoor!

"Everything happen in Indiuh," said the driver, with remorseless delight. He wagged his head vigorously. "Terrible great country."

He grinned at the mirror and Annie grinned back. That was enough. She raised a solitary thumb to the rear-vision mirror in recognition of his wisdom. She did not need to tell him about her experience. It had happened before, many times.

About the Author

AUSTRALIAN WRITER-DIPLOMAT BRUCE GRANT HAS written ten works of non-fiction, three novels, essays and short stories published in *The New Yorker*, *Mademoiselle*, *Playboy*, *Cleo*, *The Bulletin*, *Quadrant*, *Overland* and *Meanjin*. His first book, *Indonesia*, became a classic. *The Last Kiss* is one of three novels on the theme "Love in the Asian Century". He was a Nieman Fellow at Harvard University, Australian High Commissioner in New Delhi, foundation chairman of the Australia-Indonesia Institute, chairman of the Australian Dance Theatre, chairman of the Victorian Premier's Literary Awards, president of Melbourne's International Film Festival and president of Melbourne's International Arts Festival. His essay "The Great Pretender at the Bar of Justice", written at the trial of Slobodan Milosevic, was published in *The Best Australian Essays 2002*. "Bali: The Spirit of Here and Now", written after the October 2002 bombings, was published in *The Best Australian Essays 2004*. He was awarded the degree of Doctor of Letters (*honoris causa*) by Monash University in December 2003 and distinguished Fellow by the Australian Institute of International Affairs in 2010.